Angel took the paper. He read, " 'Tina. The Coffee Spot.' "

"Nice-looking girl," Doyle supplied. "Needs help."

Angel frowned slightly. "I don't get it. How am I supposed to know what she—"

"You get involved, remember?" Doyle gestured. "Get into her life."

"Why would a woman I've never even met talk to me?"

Doyle looked at him askance. "Have you looked in the mirror lately?" He paused. "No, I guess you really haven't."

"I'm not good with people."

Doyle said, "Well, that's the point of this little exercise, isn't it? Get to know her. If you can help her, you'll both be the better for it. You game?"

ANGEL

city of

A novelization of the series premiere
By Nancy Holder
Based on the teleplay by
David Greenwalt & Joss Whedon
Based on the television series created by
Joss Whedon & David Greenwalt

POCKET PULSE

New York   London   Toronto   Sydney   Singapore

This book is a work of fiction. Names, characters, places and incidents are products of the author's imagination or are used fictitiously. Any resemblance to actual events or locales or persons, living or dead, is entirely coincidental.

An *Original* Publication of POCKET BOOKS

POCKET PULSE published by
Pocket Books, a division of Simon & Schuster Inc.
1230 Avenue of the Americas, New York, NY 10020

™ and copyright © 1999 by Twentieth Century Fox Film Corporation. All rights reserved.

ISBN: 0-671-04144-4

First Pocket Pulse printing December 1999

10 9 8 7 6 5 4 3 2 1

POCKET PULSE and colophon are registered trademarks of Simon & Schuster Inc.

Printed in the U.S.A.

For Maryelizabeth Hart
and
Jeff Mariotte

with love

Acknowledgments

With sincere thanks and appreciation to the cast and crew of *Angel*, especially Joss Whedon, David Greenwalt, Caroline Kallas, and of course, David Boreanaz; to Debbie Olshan at Fox; to my wonderful Pocket family: Lisa Clancy, Micol Ostow, and Liz Shiflett; to my agent and friend, Howard Morhaim, and his assistant, Lindsay Sagnette. As always, thanks to Chris. My gratitude to Stinne Lighthart and Karen Hackett; and to my baby-sitters: Ida Khabazian, Bekah and Julie Simpson, Julie Cross, and April and Lara Koljonen.

ANGEL

city of

For Peace, Wherever He May Find Her

"You have no idea what it's like to have done the things I've done, and to care."

—Angel

In shadow, on a rooftop, Angel stood alone. He scanned the vast starfield below that was the city of Los Angeles. L.A.: a glittering matrix of hopes and dreams and wishes, some of which would soon be granted to the lucky few. Good things happened, and not only to good people. Fate herself performed random acts of kindness. Tonight careers would be made, people would fall in love forever, babies would be born.

Sometimes, God sent his angels.

But sometimes, unimaginable horrors dug themselves out of the underground and devoured the innocent. The monsters came, and they took you.

You could fight, or beg, or pray, and they took you anyway. You could be good, and honest, and self-

1

sacrificing, shielding your loved ones and crying, "Take me instead of her!"

And so they did.

Standing atop the glittering skyscraper, Angel didn't know why he had come back to Los Angeles. All he had known was that he had to get out of Sunnydale, the little town on a hellmouth also known to its original Spanish settlers as *Boca del Infierno*—the mouth of Hell.

And it had been the mouth of Hell for him, in more ways than one. Buffy had sent him to Hell herself, with a sword and with a kiss.

For her he would go to Hell forever. His need for the Slayer, the Chosen One of all her generation, had grown to the point where he wanted Buffy Anne Summers more than he wanted his soul. For one more night in her arms he was willing to be damned forever. Just to know her touch, feel her sigh . . .

What was a millennium of torture, compared to that precious single instant of paradise?

The glittering landscape twinkled back at him. He closed his eyes as memories washed through him. He had not expected to be so overtaken by the past in this city of tomorrow. His nights were dominated with vivid images of his long life; by day, his mind spun fever dreams.

He stood on the rooftop, staring down at the city. Someone else might think he was watching over the rush and swirl of humanity that was L.A.

Someone might think he was tireless, yet he was drained to the core. Seemingly in command, and yet at the mercy of forces not yet understood.

Angel wasn't aware that on another rooftop, someone watched him. His name was Doyle, and what he saw was the strangest thing—to him—on this vast plain of existence: a vampire with a soul. As far as he knew, Angel was the only one of his demonic kind with his humanity restored to him.

In Doyle's mind, that made Angel an intensely tragic figure.

Also, a hero.

A victim.

But a victor.

A man with a burden.

And a purpose.

A man who, when he looked out over his new city, must surely muse about how he lived, how he died, and how on earth he kept on going.

How on earth, indeed, Doyle thought.

"I can walk like a man. But I'm not one."

That's what Angel had once told Buffy.

So what am I? Angel wondered. *What am I now?*

He watched the city.

He watched until dawn.

PROLOGUE

Another night.

Another thousand memories.

Los Angeles. It's a city like no others, Angel thought. *And like all others.*

In the dying sun, glass skyscrapers shone like 8×10 glossies, the kind the talent agencies sent out by the gross to casting agents all over the valley: attractive faces with shiny, happy smiles. *Come on in; I've got the goods.*

With a brief smile he found himself remembering Buffy's terror when she and her two best friends, Willow Rosenberg and Xander Harris, were forced to perform in the Sunnydale High School talent show. He had fought by her side as she reduced a gang of vampires to piles of dust without so much as a grunt. But when faced with a typical teenage-girl terror, she had been, well, a typical teenage girl.

Angel drove the streets in his convertible, trying to make Los Angeles familiar again. With the rest of the traffic he crawled down the ultra-luxe strip mall that was Rodeo Drive. To his right were the famous white statues of tourists taking pictures of each other; at the end of the lane sprawled the hotel in which Eddie Murphy's character had stayed in *Beverly Hills Cop*.

The shoppers—the real ones—were pearlescent, truly beautiful to look at. Couples, moms, girlfriends prowling in packs, they were dressed in the height of fashion, in clothes that fit perfectly. For the most part, they looked unflappable. Relaxed, in calm control, nothing in their demeanor betraying the slightest bit of concern about anything in their lives.

Mere blocks away Beverly Hills sprawled, with its enormous, beautiful homes. Lucille Ball's house was so big it had two street addresses. Some of the palatial residences had been in movies—the Greystoke mansion came to mind; some were actual movie sets—the "witch's house" he occasionally passed.

These were the people for whom the Hollywood dream had become reality. It happened. And for some, wealth and fame were even better than they'd imagined they would be.

Against the smudged sky, people were going home. The wide boulevards of Beverly Hills swelled with Range Rovers, stretch limos, and tour buses.

The traffic was ungodly. Angel had read that there were more Mercedes Benzes per capita in Southern California than anywhere else in the United States. Only locals had the nerve to make a left across the lanes of traffic, even when they had the light. Even when their cars were worth half a million dollars.

Or when, like Angel, they figured they would live forever.

Mass trans was for bottom feeders. By car, sad and dirty Western Boulevard was not all that far from Beverly Hills. Any kid who had ever been in a high school play could hitch from the hellacious bus station to the nearest Avis, rent a Porsche, and try to bolt the famous baroque gates of the Paramount lot.

Driving south, he reached some of the sad, bad parts of town. Here there was poverty. Here dreams had died. In the twilight some weatherworn pages of *The Hollywood Reporter* snapped against a chain-link fence. Hip-hop made the windows of a two-story stucco house shake, rattle, and roll. Little kids played tag among the tumbleweeds and crushed Colt .45 cans. Billy D's, they were called. But there weren't many lying around: They could be turned in for money. There was a lot of recycling going down here. A lot of things turned in for a few coins: glass, newspapers, blood, and friends with outstanding warrants.

Angel supposed it was understandable. A few

coins would buy something to eat: a taco, a can of cat food. Or something to drink: a Pepsi, a bottle of Thunderbird. Or an escape: a ticket to whatever was playing at the dollar theaters.

A ticket to whatever was available to shoot into your arm.

These were the Angelenos he supposed in some ways were most like him. Isolated. Wary. They figured that friends would leave you eventually; either because you didn't measure up, or they died, or they got thrown in jail. If your friend didn't hurt you, you would probably hurt your friend.

So it was best not to make any.

Best to stay guarded and protected and as safe as possible, because the world was a great, big, dangerous minefield.

Only in his case, he was the minefield.

Last week a family of ten living in a one-bedroom in Compton had lost their lives in a fire. They were from Guatemala, and six of them supported the others by working illegally, for half the legal minimum wage, in a Chinese restaurant.

Most people did not come to L.A. with hopes of making it big in the drug trade. They just wanted to make it, period.

But some did come for the easy, dirty score. Crips, Bloods, Hell's Angels, the Asian tongs, the Japanese *yakuza*. Los Angeles was the Pacific Rim's doorway to American crime: Give me your degenerate, your psychopathic, yearning to make millions.

Angel drove south to Culver City, where Sony had its movie lot. It was a huge dream factory. He'd overheard that across the street, Atlanta had been burned for *Gone With the Wind*. Actually, old sets from other films had gone up in flames.

Every once in a while there was a terrible accident on a set: Stuntmen got maimed for life, actors got killed. Like in *Twilight Zone*. Like in *The Crow*. But like plane crashes, those were the stories the media picked up. For the most part, stunt people came out of their "gags" with nothing more than bruises.

Immortal, like Angel.

As the darkness rose, Los Angeles began its waking dreams. The girls who mud-wrestled at the Tropicana dreamed of finding some rich guy who would forget their sleazy roots, or getting cast as an extra in a low-budget horror movie. It often happened, but, as far as Angel could tell, it didn't make a lasting change in their lives.

The waiters and store clerks on Melrose, where funky street wear and great bookstores mingled with fetish shops and themed chain restaurants, dreamed of finding a manager, getting a speaking role, landing that all important S.A.G. card. It happened often enough to keep all the other waiters and store clerks gainfully underemployed, working for that big break.

The UCLA film-school students dreamed of being the next Cameron or Eszterhas. All it took was for that to happen once in a generation to keep the flame alive.

Where else could dreaming lift you from parking cars to directing Cruise in less time than it took to earn a college degree? It didn't mean you were the best, or the most talented, or even the most persistent. It meant you had the best luck.

Los Angeles was a city more obsessed with luck than any other city in the world, including Las Vegas, Reno, and Atlantic City.

That was the thrill of it. There was no way to control luck. No way to court it. No way to avoid it.

That was why Los Angeles ground the unlucky up, ground them down, and wiped them out.

But it was also why Los Angeles could be a most generous oasis of good karma. Rub two nickels together—make a contact here, another there—and you might be set for life. Lots of money, intelligent friends, work you cared about—that could happen in Los Angeles, too.

It has a hundred faces, each different, each one beckoning, Angel thought, driving.

In the poor neighborhoods such as Watts, Little Saigon, and East L.A., he saw terrified boy hustlers with skin the color of cocoa butter; girls in magenta hair and whiteface, hiding the needle tracks thick as the stems of black roses when the cop cars prowled near.

In Hollywood proper, the police tried to keep the streets clear. But there you found bums of all stripes, drinking, staggering, begging. The homeless, giving the streets a bad name and hogging all the cardboard. The druggies, forgetting which clinic was open when and getting confused and trying to sneak inside the beautifully restored Roosevelt Hotel to use their toilets.

But cheek by jowl with the unlucky were the excited, energetic up-and-comers with cell phones and Palm Pilots, nicely dressed and dropping the right names: Steven, Leo, Angelina. People who knew the right people.

People who *were* the right people.

Such contradictions. Such texture and confusion.

People are drawn here. People, and other things. They come for all kinds of reasons. My reason? It started with a girl.

"A really, really pretty girl," Angel slurred.

There was a glass in front of him; he was seated in Sector 1.8 on the blood alcohol hit parade; the serious drinkers surrounded him, totally ignoring him, throwing back whatever worked to the heartbeat of

America: the edgy throb of young urban success. Artists from the downtown lofts; young professionals doing the networking thing; unemployed actors looking to drown their sorrows in each other's arms. Or somewhere. For free, even.

The city, dreaming that 70-millimeter dream.

"No, I mean she was a hottie girl," Angel ran on.

No one around him cared that he had loved Buffy the Vampire Slayer back in beautiful Sunnydale-on-the-hellmouth any more now than they had two minutes ago. Maybe because he didn't tell them that Buffy Anne Summers had been her name, and that she had been the Chosen One—the one girl in all her generation summoned to fight the vampires, demons, and forces of darkness.

Maybe because he didn't mention that he had nearly killed her twice; and that when he left her, he took one last, long look, but he had never said good-bye.

Nor was anyone impressed that he was one of a kind, even among his own kind: Angel was the only vampire in existence with a soul. You'd think that would be cause for a free round or two.

Of course, to be fair, no one in the bar knew he was a vampire. When he wasn't in feeding mode—or really pissed off—he looked like your average tall, dark, and unusually pale Southern California guy. On occasion, people had been startled by how cold his pale skin was; which made sense, since he was technically dead.

For the rest of the vampire population, what they were was a demon inhabiting the shell of a corpse. The soul of the deceased was gone. Maybe fled to heaven. Who knew? Angel had only ever been to Hell. In his case, the demon inside him had to endure the presence of his soul, making Angel's existence so much more complicated than the average bloodsucker's.

Lonelier, frankly.

And speaking of the joy, one other thing was for certain: Vampires could, and did, get drunk. Hell, Angel's ex-hunting buddy Spike had set records when he was trying to get over his faithless lover, Drusilla. And as Spike had amply demonstrated, vampires also had hangovers the next day . . . and nasty burns, if they passed out where the morning sunlight could fall across them.

Burns healed fast, though. It was the other wounds—the ones that didn't show—the ones inside—that took longer to mend.

Seemed like forever.

Ah, well.

"She had . . . her hair was . . . you know, you kind of remind me of her," Angel said unsteadily.

The large black man seated next to him made no comment. He just kept drinking.

" 'Cause, you know, the hair. I mean, you both have hair."

And drinking.

A woman's laugh drew Angel's gaze back to the three guys shooting pool with two good-looking young women. There it was, the pang: One of them looked a little bit like Buffy. Of course, he saw Buffy everywhere. He could see her face on a blank wall the way some people saw the Virgin Mary in a tortilla.

The balls clacked as they played. One of the pool guys came over to the bar and squeezed in next to Angel. He had a fifty in his hand like it was a dollar. Beer breath and aftershave collided as he said to the bartender, "We're gonna cash out."

Angel grinned at him. "Girls are nice."

The guy gave him a look of contempt, got his change, and split.

The group gathered up and moved past Angel, heading out the back exit. Angel swiveled slowly around on his stool, watching them. As soon as he was out of their line of vision, his entire demeanor shifted. His eyes went cold and purposeful, and his loopy expression became serious, focused. He was extremely alert.

Yeah, vampires could get drunk.

But Angel was stone cold sober.

He followed the jovial group outside, a man on a

mission, to the parking lot behind the bar. The lot was fairly dark, and very deserted. The girl who had laughed—the one who looked like Buffy—was chattering excitedly to Mr. Fifty Bucks.

She said, "You guys really know the doorman, you can get us in the Lido?"

The guy shrugged.

"I don't want to go clubbing anymore." He threw an arm around her, leered, pawed a little. "I want to party right here."

He made it clear what kind of party he was talking about. Angel kept his distance, but he stayed light on the balls of his feet. He'd known for at least two hours what was eventually going to go down. Here it was, and he was ready.

The girl wasn't pleased by her date's mauling. "Hey, *back off.*"

" 'Hey,' " the guy flung back at her, "shut up and *die.*"

And just as Angel had expected him to, the guy growled and morphed into a hideous, yellow-eyed, fang-toothed vampire. It grabbed the girl as its buddies morphed and grabbed her friend.

The women were too freaked even to scream as Angel stumbled toward them, apparently snockered.

" 'Scusey, 'scusey, anybody seen my car? It's big and shiny." He looked around stupidly. "Why does it keep doing this to me?"

The vampire with the cash kept to the shadows as it warned Angel, "Piss off, pal."

Angel stumbled up to the guy. He looked up at the vampire and registered drunken shock at its face. Frowning, Angel dug in his coat pocket and pulled out some dental floss.

"No," he assured the vamp very earnestly, "I want you to have it."

The vampire shoved the girl to the side. She hit her head against the parking lot wall.

Fang guy went for Angel, who decided it was time to drop the drunk act; he whipped his elbow up under its chin, knocking him clean over a car as the second of the three vamps charged. Angel got in a good spin kick, just before number three clocked him.

Angel and the third one traded vicious blows. The fight was brutal, savage, and over as Angel sent the vampire crashing into a pile of garbage, splintering some boxes in the fall.

The girl held her bleeding head as she and her girlfriend watched the carnage.

The second vampire got to its feet and charged. Vampire see, vampire do: Number three was no more original than his fangmates.

Angel stood, waiting calmly and efficiently as they rushed him from either side. He held his hands down behind his back and loosened his secret weapons.

Two sharp wooden stakes, attached to wooden spring devices on his wrists, ratcheted into his hands. He shot his arms out to either side, nailing both his adversaries at the same time.

Also simultaneously the two exploded in shrieking fireworks of dust.

Angel de-ratcheted his stakes. He picked up the sound of footsteps behind him and swung around as the last remaining vampire reared up with a metal trash can and smashed Angel in the face with it. It was not so much the pain as the pressure—that was what he told himself anyway—but he had a feeling he was going to be scraping metal off his teeth for at least a week.

Angel hit the ground, hard, his back to the two girls.

Now he was pissed off.

"You shouldn't have done that," he said to the trash-can vampire.

He went vampfaced as he grabbed his attacker. The other guy obviously had not realized Angel was one of his own—with slight modifications. Even now it was clear that he was confused.

Angel took advantage. He wailed on it, taking everything out on it; giving it holy hell, beating it to a bloody pulp before he flung it headfirst into the windshield of a fine European automobile. It knocked the monster out and set off the car alarm.

For a moment the only sound was the squeal of the alarm. Then the girl ran up behind Angel.

"Oh, my god, you saved our lives," she said, gasping and shuddering.

Angel kept his back to the girls—to the one who had spoken, and to her friend, who looked like Buffy.

"Go home," he said gruffly.

But the girl was not to be deterred. She dashed after him as her shock began to set back in.

"They were . . . oh, god . . . thank you—"

She grabbed his arm and pulled him around.

He still wore his true face.

His monster face.

A trickle of blood from her head wound edged down her neck. Angel's vampire senses honed in on it, compelled him, pushed, taunted.

"Get away from me." She would not recognize it as an agonized plea.

She started violently; quickly she backed away with her friend in tow.

Grimly Angel strode away as the girls clambered into their car. Without breaking stride, he grabbed a broken stake from the trash and dusted the semiconscious vampire sprawled on the hood of the Mercedes.

He morphed back. Now he was just another guy walking down the nightstreets of Los Angeles.

Walking into shadow.

Remembering way too much . . . about how he got there, on that long and winding road. . . .

THE FALL

Galway, Ireland, 1753

Angelus was not in a good humor.

In fact, he was in the worst of humors.

His village, the Irish village of Galway, had nothing to recommend itself, sure and not for one of the gentry such as himself, one Master Angelus, eldest son of the family, and bored beyond withstanding.

He stomped the streets in a lather, never minding who knew. Though the streets were crowded, it was with people of no consequence: shoemakers and gossips, old women who had the temerity to smoke their long pipes on the streets. Barefoot children—so many everywhere—watching the basketmaker pushing his sally rods into the loam to start a fresh weave for an oyster basket.

A surfeit of monotony; an excess of ordinariness.

Angelus was certain that the larger Irish cities—or even better, the English ones—held wonders denied folk of commoner towns and villages.

Never mind that his heart told him to run away. And forbear, all ye Saints, that he should dare to steal even one moment from his studies to sketch the face of a lovely peasant wench. His father was sure to be up in arms again, nattering on about the tuition money and where was the money for the cart he was to have procured?

It was moot now that Taffy Maclise had sworn on the honor of his betrothed that his horse could not lose, due to the fact that he had fed the creature a marvelous new concoction to lend it the speed of Mercury himself.

Cheating, some may call it. A sure thing, Taffy had insisted. But sure, and not sure enough: The nag had come in dead last. And then died, not to put too fine a point on it.

"And this night he'll discover his own sweetheart, Brigid O'Donnel, in bed with another man," Angelus muttered as he trudged down by the quay.

Then he smiled to himself.

And I'll be the man to tup dear Brigid, he thought. Then he dismissed the thought as beneath him. She were a lady, and not the common sort he had taken to visiting. Even he had a few scruples left.

Besides, she was dark-headed, and he so did like the fairer ladies. Like Bess, his favorite, down at Mistress Burton's Society House. It was a place no decent young gentleman would find himself . . . or rather, allow himself to be found.

Had he a piece of silver, he would spend it there this very night. He needed a bit of cheer—a pint in his drinking mug, a wench on his knee . . . and then even Galway could be bearable.

He was quayside now. The stink of fish rose strong and unforgettable. Fishing nets and masts reminded him of spiderwebs and spider's legs, wrapping him up to feed off him later—once he finished school.

That was a doom if ever there was one.

"Angelus, me boyo!"

It was Sandy Burns, coming up from the fishing boats. He was Angelus's favorite friend in all the world. The young man was natty-dressed in the very latest and already surveying the fishing fleet he would some day inherit from his uncle.

Angelus smiled and gave him a wave, slowing so that Sandy could catch up.

"It's a blessing that I found you," Sandy told him, slightly out of breath. "Your father's got a letter from old Nicholl." That being Paddy Nicholl, the schoolmaster. "And he's out looking for you with a horsewhip in his fist."

Angelus sighed. "Of that I've no doubt. The meaning of which is, I cannot go home tonight." He smiled at his friend. "Have you any money, Sandy? We can go and dine at Mistress Burton's."

Sandy laughed. "Me thoughts exactly, Angelus! I've a bit of money, but not a lot. Let's game it up, see what we can win. And then you'll have your Bess."

"Done, and done," Angelus said, laughing. "I've a yen for faro. I play that game like a wizard, I do."

"Sure, and that's true," Sandy agreed. "We'll have enough money for all the girls at Mistress Burton's."

"Just give me Bess," Angelus said.

"A romantic, at your age," Sandy chided.

The two friends went off.

And by dark they were fortune's fools. Drink and bad wagers had devoured Sandy's small purse. Bess was pouting and eager, but Angelus had not a penny in his pocket.

At that, Mistress Burton's doorman, Old Tim, had thrown the two youths out, grumbling about deadbeats.

That was when Angelus caught the notion to steal his father's table silver. Sandy went along with it, and they were off to do the deed.

But then the whiskey caught up with Sandy, and he lay in the street as drunk as a field hand on payday.

So Angelus bade him good night and wobbled on down the road himself.

That was when he saw her.

She was a lady, obviously of means, dressed in the height of fashion. He could almost hear the rustle of her silks and satins.

The jingle of coins in her purse.

The lilt of her voice as she sighed.

She headed alone into a dark alley. A gentleman he was: Concerned only for her safety, of course, he followed after. He was weaving slightly, but surely she would take no mind. He was young, and young men drink of an evening.

She stood in moonlight, and she was beautiful. A fair-headed woman in a ball gown, her lovely figure amply displayed.

His heart swelled and he approached, and she kept her ground, waiting for him.

He asked her what a lady of such station was doing unaccompanied in such a place.

She was coy, speaking of loneliness. Challenging him with words and glances to be bold.

He took up that gauntlet, aye, most eagerly.

And then she promised to show him the world, if only he would be brave. He was fair crazed with lust and the passion she promised.

She moved to him and touched his chest. His heart was pounding. She told him to close his eyes.

He did it.

In that moment he left Galway forever. He left the world behind.

Her teeth found his neck and tore it open, and she drank of him. He was frozen, locked in pain; unable to move, to cry out, to resist in any way.

As when she drew her nail across her own chest and held his face to her breast. Made him drink.

At first he was like to retch. But the taste . . . there was something in her blood; a magick, a power; she was a fairy, he decided, a changeling, a queen of the beyond . . . His young man's heart pounded; his young man's body thrummed with the thrill and the fear and the danger. He knew himself to be sore in danger of something bitter and demonic. It were a mortal danger; if he did not leave off this drinking of her, he would die more than once: His soul would die.

Deep inside himself, he knew this. He knew it and kept drinking.

And knew something else: That at one point as she had drunk of him, she would have let him go. He felt her grip relax, just slightly. Felt the sharp teeth raise a few breadths from his vein. It was his last chance. He knew it clearer than anything old Paddy Nicholl had ever schooled him in.

But his answer to the imperilment of his soul was this: He held her more tightly, urging her on. Perhaps later he would tell himself it was because she was so fair and lovely; or because her skin was like alabaster; or that her perfume had intoxicated him. That she had enchanted him to it.

Allowing her to defile him so was an unholy thing, but it was *something more,* something beyond schoolmasters and whores and getting drunk and playing whist and faro. It was past his experience, which made him all the hungrier for it to go on and on, until his soul fled to heaven . . . or, if his father were to be believed, straight to the everlasting fires of Hell.

His da was a big one for standing up for yourself. If you permitted bodily harm upon your person, you so much as did it yourself. Better to die of this a suicide than to grow old and doddering, mired in excruciating ordinariness.

So now he gulped down her blood, drawing it in hungrily as a statement that this was his choice. Though he couldn't stop his drinking, he told himself that he *wouldn't* stop. That it was his decision.

But the truth he would need one day was this: He couldn't stop.

Her name was Darla, and she changed him into a vampire. She was his sire.

In his new world of shadow she became his constant companion, his mistress, his tempting, dark paramour. They ran together for centuries, hunting and playing, and she taught him the fierce, savage joy of what they were. The world of a thousand nights lay at their feet, and they were twin comets, soaring across fields, moors, and white cliffs, burning everything they touched.

What a universe! What a marvel! It was a glorious existence. It was more than he, a poorly-schooled lad from Galway, could ever have dreamed of, and there was nothing he wouldn't do for Darla in order to repay her generosity.

All she asked of him was his company, which he was glad to give.

His life became sheer ecstasy.

Until it went so very wrong.

ACT ONE

> "One hell of a city, man. Buckets of fun if you're a nasty creature of some kind. A little hard on the humans. People get very lost; they get very dead and worse. Everyone's got their demons."
>
> —Doyle

Darla, my sire.

I killed her to save Buffy.

The ultimate sin for a vampire to commit. Yet I didn't hesitate.

Angel had been thinking about Darla for a couple nights. He found it within himself to mourn her. He knew what it was like to be changed; and as he had reminded himself before, she, too, had known a vampire's fatal kiss and been transformed by it. The vampires who walked the night were hybrids of the Old Ones—the demons who had ruled the world

27

before the coming of humanity—and of humankind itself. Darla had once been a lovely blond-haired girl.

Someone like Buffy.

No. Nobody was like Buffy.

In Los Angeles the streets of legitimate businesses rolled up early. Despite gossip in the tabloids, even the clubs catering to the young set were pretty much deserted by midnight. Actors had lines to learn, and they had to report for makeup and hair with the sunrise. Not surprisingly, the rhythm of the city revolved around "the talent."

West Coast big-money players—the ones who ultimately supplied the talent with paychecks—had to stay current with financial markets all over the world—the Nikkei in Japan, the Bourse in Paris, and the New York Stock Exchange, to name but a few. So they were up at the crack of dawn—up at all hours—making trades and gathering valuable information. Like serious, working entertainment stars, they were early to bed, early to rise, and as a result, wealthy.

The late hours belonged to those who would never, ever hear a wake-up call: druggies, runaways, plain old bums. So did the strip joints, the dives, and the crack houses.

Angel walked past the hollow faces, keeping to himself like everybody else. He turned up a smaller street, which was a mix of old residential and small commercial buildings. Rumor had it that Nathaniel West, author of *The Day of the Locust,* had once lived around here. Angel didn't know if that was true, but he'd read the novel. It was a harsh and un-relenting book about Hollywood and the grotesque lives of the neverwases who couldn't accept that the magic simply wasn't going to rub off on them.

He entered an old building in a row of old build-ings. There were old offices on the ground floor, apartments above. There was nothing inspiring or noteworthy about it.

He unlocked a door and walked inside. The office came with his apartment, but he had no need for it. He had no business, no storefront. Nevertheless, he had possession of an outer and an inner office space. Naturally, the place was forlorn and uncared-for. There was a beat-up desk, some chairs, and a couple of musty filing cabinets shoved into corners.

He had no idea what the previous tenant had used the office for; he had heard rumors that there had been some kind of boiler-room operation, a scam to persuade old people to buy aluminum sid-ing for their houses or some nonsense. At any rate, it came cheap.

Angel shoved the deadbolt into place and made sure the door was locked. He crossed through the room to the back corner and entered an old elevator.

Although the other apartments were located on the higher floors, he didn't push Up. Angel lived in the basement, farther away from the sun. It seemed that no matter where he lived, he was destined to spend a good portion of his time underground. Rather fitting, in a way. These days he felt more than dead, anyway.

He knew for a fact that many of the dead despaired. Others raged against the light.

Few were real, true zombies, mindlessly walking the tombways, stumbling around with no sense of direction.

Like him.

The elevator door opened, revealing a few more memories for Angel of Sunnydale. Some of his effects could be found in the clean and eclectically elegant space: a few of his own sketches among the tapestries and artworks. In a drawer a clutch of photographs of Buffy and her friends were turned facedown, but he knew them by heart.

A flower Buffy had once given him sat on the stack of pictures. It was faded, the petals like ash.

A bookcase held a number of arcane books such as Buffy's Watcher, Giles, used to thumb through for hours on end, trying to keep the Slayer one step ahead of her supernatural adversaries. Angel had a couple of easy chairs, for someone whose life wasn't easy.

Weapons.

He had lots of those.

He slipped off his coat and tossed it on a chair. With the semiconscious movements of one who has done something many, many times, he unfastened the two ratchet-stake devices strapped to his forearms and dropped them on a table. Other stakes, knives, and a fight ax cluttered the surface.

The vampire leaned on the table, staring at the weaponry, remembering the expressions on the faces of the girls whose lives he had saved.

Remembering Buffy, who had once told him she no longer even noticed when he looked like a demon and when he wore his human features. Who had kissed him powerfully and passionately no matter what he looked like.

Buffy . . .

Those wounds . . . when did time heal them? Because maybe he would just go to sleep for a hundred years.

Yeah, and dream of nothing but her for a century.

The dreams of Slayers often came true. What about those of vampires?

He had another flash of memory, this one about Buffy's dream that Dru would one day kill him.

He'd held her then, assured that even Slayers have honest-to-goodness nonsense nightmares. But she would have none of it.

"It was so real," she told him, and described it so completely that he felt as if he had dreamed it himself:

In her sleep Buffy stirred. She opened her eyes, registering the stillness, and turned on the light with the upside-down lampshade on her nightstand. She took a drink of water and slowly got out of bed.

Padding down the hall to the bathroom in her blue satin pajama bottoms and black tank top . . .

. . . Ah, there she is, Drusilla thought as she stepped behind the Slayer and followed her down the hall. Blood pooled in the corners of her mouth, a nice contrast to her black gown. . . .

. . . Buffy opened the door to the bathroom and in-explicably stepped into the Bronze.

Music echoed hauntingly off the walls as smiling couples glided together. There was no band. The shadowed room was dotted with spots of golden light, and everyone moved more slowly than normal. Disoriented, Buffy felt as though she were underwater. And yet, she felt herself part of the otherworldly scene, as if she didn't quite make sense, either.

Then she saw Willow, seated at a high table with a large cup of coffee on a saucer. A organ grinder's monkey in a little red cap and jacket perched beside her. Very matter-of-factly, Willow said, in French, "The hippo stole his pants."

She smiled perkily and waved at Buffy, who waved uncertainly back.

Bewildered, she moved on.

Standing by a post, her mother was drinking coffee from a cup very much like Willow's. As she lifted it to her lips, she asked her daughter, "Do you really think you're ready, Buffy?"

Buffy frowned. "What?"

The saucer slipped from Joyce's grasp. It fell to the floor and shattered. As if she didn't even notice, she blankly turned and walked away.

Again, Buffy moved on.

She was on the dance floor. Couples danced, the strange music twining around them, as Buffy wandered, alone.

Then the crowd parted.

And he was there.

Angel, she thought radiantly as the dark, mysterious vampire smiled back at her. Dressed all in black, he was the center of the room; there was light in his face, for her; he did make sense, surrounded by all these things which didn't. He was a connection; he was the connection. She felt as if he were already touching her as they walked toward each other, hands outstretched.

Then Drusilla appeared behind him. As Buffy watched in horror, the vampire stabbed him in the back.

Buffy screamed, "Angel!"

His shaking hand strained toward hers, crumbling to ashes before her eyes.

He had time to look at her, agony in his eyes—love lost, yearning, so lost—and then he exploded into dust.

Drusilla stood fully revealed, her golden eyes shining with glee.

"Happy Birthday, Buffy," she said, relishing Buffy's despair.

So far as Angel knew, Dru was still alive. Just because the dream hadn't come true yet didn't mean that it never would.

Maybe Dru would follow him to Los Angeles and kill him. Maybe that's why he was here.

Maybe the past caught up with one, sooner or later. Maybe that was why he couldn't seem to connect with the present anymore. He was simply drifting along, losing himself deeper and deeper in reminiscing, like an old man.

Suddenly he sensed that he was no longer alone. He turned slowly, well aware that he had an arsenal at his disposal.

In the doorway stood a young dark-haired man with angular features and dark eyes. He had the composure of someone who assumed he'd been expected.

He said, "Well, I like the place. Not much with the view, but it's got a nice Batcave sort of air to it."

He spoke as if they knew each other. He had an Irish accent. Angel was Irish, too. But he couldn't place this stranger to save his . . . soul.

"Who are you?"

"Doyle," the man informed him. "And, no, we haven't met before, so don't be embarrassed."

Angel frowned slightly. "I'm not." He added, "You don't smell human."

The guy—Doyle—was mildly affronted. "Well, that's a bit *rude*. As it happens I'm very much human—"

He sneezed, and instantly morphed into a blue, scaly thing. Casually he shook it off, turned human again.

"—on my mother's side. Anyway, I come in uninvited so you know I'm not a vampire like yourself."

He walked into the room, past Angel, drawn to the weapons.

Angel asked, "What do you want?"

"I've been sent," Doyle replied. "By the Powers that Be."

"By the Powers that Be What?"

"This is an exciting bunch of crimefighting devices." Doyle picked up a throwing star. "I can't believe you really know how to use these."

Angel glowered at his uninvited guest. "I'm anxious to show you."

Doyle shrugged. "Tell you something, friend: I'm

about as happy to be here as you are to see me. But there's work to be done, and we got the call." A beat. "Let me tell you a little bedtime story."

"But I'm not sleepy."

Doyle ignored him. "Once upon a time there was a vampire, and he was the meanest vampire in all the land. Other vampires were afraid of him, he was such a bastard."

His Irish lilt made it sound like a fairy tale. But Angel knew where this was going. He knew who it was about.

Himself, as they used to say in the Old Country. Probably still did.

"A hundred years this guy's killing and maiming and such like. Then one day he's cursed. By Gypsies. They restore his human soul, and all of a sudden he's mad with guilt, 'what have I done,' very freaked. So he sulks about for another hundred years—"

Angel cut him off. "Okay. I'm sleepy."

"It's a fairly dull tale," Doyle agreed thoughtfully, and Angel stirred, coming back from his reverie.

"It needs a little sex, is my feeling, and sure enough, enter the girl. Pretty little blond thing, Vampire Slayer by trade, and our vampire falls madly in love with her."

Angel wanted him to shut up. But he said nothing. There was no sense letting Doyle know he'd gotten to him. These days no one got to Angel.

Just as in Manhattan no one had gotten through to him.

Except another demon, sent for much the same reason, or so it appeared.

Manhattan, 1996

A rat a month, that's all Angel ate. He was crazed with hunger and isolation, and didn't even know it.

Then Whistler had shown, in his cheesy suit that somehow reminded Angel of bowling shirts, and dorky hat and his Queens accent, and started the conversation with a real opener:

"God, are you disgusting."

Angel jerked, completely unused to being talked to. He started to crawl back into the shadows of the alley.

"This is really an unforgettable smell," Whistler continued. "This is the stench of death you're giving off here. And the look says Crazy Homeless Guy." He shook his head. "It's not good."

"Get away from me."

Whistler feigned terror. "What are you gonna do, bite me? Oh, horrors! A vampire!"

Angel stared at him. He had no idea who this person was, or how he knew what Angel was. But he did know.

"Oh, but you're not gonna bite me because of

your poor tortured *soul*," Whistler continued, mocking him. "It's so sad, a vampire with a soul. How poignant. I may physically vomit right here."

"Who are you?" Angel demanded.

"A demon, technically. But I'm not a bad guy. Not all demons are dedicated to the destruction of all life. Someone has to maintain balance, you know. Good and evil can't exist without each other, blah blah blah. I'm not like a good fairy or anything. I'm just trying to make it all balance. Do I come off defensive?"

Angel had no answer for that. But Whistler had plenty more to say.

"You could become an even more useless rodent than you are right now, or you could become . . . someone. A *person*. Someone to be counted."

Angel's voice was filled with self-loathing "I just want to be left alone." He meant it, truly. Yet he couldn't help wondering how this demon had found him, and why. Maybe it was self-preservation, and maybe it was egotistical curiosity. He wasn't sure.

"You've been alone for what, ninety years? And what an impressive package you are. The stink guy." Whistler wrinkled his nose.

Angel was the one who came off defensive. "You don't know what I have to deal with. What I've done."

Whistler rolled his eyes and sighed. "You're annoying me! The self-pity thing is not gonna bring in the chicks. It's a bore."

Knowing he was playing right into the hands of the obnoxious stranger, Angel asked, "What do you want from me?"

Whistler was clearly pleased. "I want you to see something. It's happening very soon. We'd need to leave now. You see, and then you tell me what you want to do."

What Angel saw was Buffy, a bit younger than when they finally met. Different in some way, very much the same in others. She was popular, surrounded by cute, superficial girls who could have been clones of hers. They were chatting and laughing about boys and clothes.

Until Merrick arrived.

Merrick had been her first Watcher. The man had told her of her destiny: one girl in every generation is the Chosen One; she and she alone will fight the demons, the vampires, and the forces of darkness. She is the Slayer.

She had not believed Merrick. But then he had taken her to a graveyard and shown her a few basic fight maneuvers. That very night she dusted her first vamp.

She'd come home late without calling, and had to lie about it; and as she listened in the bathroom with tears streaming down her face, her parents argued about what a terrible job each was doing raising her.

Whistler stated the obvious, but it was exactly what Angel was thinking.

"She's gonna have it tough, that Slayer. She's just a kid. And the world is full of big bad things."

Angel was filled with concern. "I want to help her," he said sincerely. "I want to . . . I want to become someone. I want to help."

Even then, Whistler had gotten off one last jab.

"Jeez, look at you. She must be prettier than the last Slayer."

Angel looked down. He had killed Slayers in his day. Whistler must know that.

"It's not gonna be easy. The more you live in the world, the more you see how apart from it you are," Whistler warned him. "And this is dangerous work. Right now you couldn't go three rounds with a fruit fly."

Angel accepted his cutting remarks. He wanted to help that young girl. "I want to learn from you."

"Okay."

They walked together. Then Angel said, "But I don't want to dress like you."

Whistler had acted mildly insulted. "See? Again you're annoying me."

"And it's good," Doyle proclaimed, bringing Angel out of his reverie and back to the present. "He makes something of himself, fights some evil, but then, eventually, the two of them, they get fleshy with one another, and the moment he . . . well, the technical term is *perfect happiness*."

He looked at Angel. "And as soon as our boy gets there, he goes bad again. Kills again. It's ugly. So when he gets his soul back a second time, he figures he can't be anywhere near young Miss Puppy Thighs without endangering them both."

Angel kept his face a mask. It was all there, the whole, sad story. His story.

His and Buffy's story.

"So he takes off. Goes to L.A., to fight evil and atone for his crimes. He's a shadow, a faceless champion of the hapless human race. Have you got a beer of any kind in here?"

Angel said flatly, "No."

Doyle was clearly skeptical. "You must have something besides pig's blood."

He went to Angel's fridge and peered inside.

"Okay, you've told me the story of my life which, since I was there, I already knew. Why aren't I kicking you out?" Angel demanded.

Empty-handed, the demon closed the fridge.

"'Cause now I'm gonna tell you what happens next. See this vampire, he thinks he's helpin'. Fighting the demons, keeping away from the humans so as not to be tempted." He gestured at the apartment. "Doing penance in his little cell."

He walked toward Angel, never taking his eyes off him.

"But he's cut off. From everything. From the people he's helping; they're not people to him at all, they're just the victims, statistics. Just numbers."

"I still save them. Who cares if I don't stop to chat?" His voice was harsh; he hated his own defensiveness. But he was irritated. *And tired and a bit . . .*

"When was the last time you drank blood?" Doyle asked abruptly.

. . . unnerved.

Angel said nothing. There was nothing he had any interest in saying.

But Doyle already knew the answer.

"It was her. Your Slayer friend. Muffy, is it?"

Despite himself, Angel answered. "I was sick. Dying. She fed me to cure me."

And I nearly killed her, he thought. *I put her in the hospital from the blood loss. I almost drank her dry.*

Doyle moved on. "Left you with a bit of a craving, didn't it? Well, that craving is gonna grow. And someday soon one of those helpless victims you don't really care about will look too appetizing to turn down. And you'll figure, 'What's one against all I've saved? I might as well eat 'em; I'm still ahead by the numbers.'"

Doyle stared Angel down, and Angel's mind filled

with the image of the blood edging down the neck of the girl he had saved tonight. True, the hunger had swept over him, so strong he had felt dizzy. But he had resisted.

But he had also known, deep down, that there would come a time when he wouldn't resist. He'd known it then, and he'd known it before.

Sometimes he woke up dreaming about feeding off Buffy.

And what would that be like, dreaming such a thing for a hundred years? Mingled passion and nightmare, from which he couldn't wake up?

Doyle changed the mood. "Come on. I'm parched from all this yakkin'. Let's go treat me to a Billy D."

A short time later Angel and his new demon friend left the twenty-four hour liquor store. Doyle was drinking a forty-ounce malt liquor in a paper bag.

"Ah, that's a good drink," he said, with deep satisfaction. "I will pay you back. I'm just a little pressed for cash this week."

Yeah, probably every week, Angel figured. Doyle looked so comfortable on the streets that Angel found himself wondering why none of the demons who came to him like the Ghosts of Christmas Past ever had any class.

"So what do I do?" he said now to Doyle. "I assume you came here with some alternative. How do I change things?"

"You got to mix it up," Doyle informed him. "Get in there with the humans. It's not all fighting and gadgets and such."

A panhandling woman approached them as Doyle waxed on, warming to his subject.

"It's about reaching out to people, caring about them, about showing them there's hope in this world—" He glared at the woman and said, "Get a job, you lazy sow." Then he turned back to Angel and added, "About letting them in your heart."

He looked almost mischievous. "You frightened yet?"

Angel said, "I want to know who sent you."

Doyle shrugged. "I'm honestly not sure. They don't speak to me direct. I get visions, which is to say great splitting migraines that come with pictures. A name, a face. I don't know who sends 'em. I just know whoever it is is more powerful than you or me, and they're trying to make things right."

It sounded familiar. It sounded like what Whistler had told him. Still, Angel wasn't sure he was going to buy anything in this particular delicatessen.

"Why me?"

Doyle said simply, " 'Cause you got potential. And the balance sheet ain't exactly in your favor just yet."

True.

"Why you?"

The demon suddenly became serious. "We all got something to atone for."

There was a silence. Angel waited. More silence. He let it drop.

Then Doyle became all business again, fishing a piece of paper out of his pocket.

"Had a vision this morning. When the blinding pain stopped, I wrote this down."

Angel took the paper. He read, " 'Tina. The Coffee Spot.' "

"Nice-looking girl," Doyle supplied. "Needs help."

Despite himself, Angel was intrigued. "Help with what?"

Doyle shrugged. "That's your business. I just get the names."

Angel frowned slightly. "I don't get it. How am I supposed to know what she—"

"You get involved, remember?" Doyle gestured. "Get into her life."

"Why would a woman I've never met even talk to me?"

Doyle looked at him askance. "Have you looked in a mirror lately?" He must have caught himself; Angel, being a vampire, cast no reflection. "No," he said, "I guess you really haven't."

Angel paused. Okay, he knew what he had to do. *But still* . . .

"I'm not good with people."

Doyle said, "Well, that's the point of this little exercise, isn't it? Get to know her. If you can help her, you'll both be the better for it. You game?"

Game?

As in, back in the game?

Thanks to "the Powers that Be," and an Irish demon with terrible taste in beers?

ACT ONE,
CONTINUED

After Doyle left, the night seemed to speed by. Lights blurred together as Angel tried to make sense of everything that had happened. The sun roared like a volcano into the sky, dawn an explosion which reminded him of the way his kind exploded when they were staked.

He stayed indoors as the day wore on. Sluggish with the need to rest, he found that everything from the night before took on an air of unreality; he half-expected the slip of paper to disappear as he studied it for a long moment, then tossed it on the bed table.

He remembered when he had talked Buffy into getting reinvolved with the battle. He had been the messenger then.

Her Doyle.

Sunnydale, 1997

He had been waiting for her to show. After Whistler revealed Buffy Summers to Angel in Los Angeles, he had been watching for her arrival.

In the brief year that had passed, she looked much older, more mature. Or perhaps that was simply because she was unhappy: She had assumed that with the move from Los Angeles, she would be free of her Slayer duties. But Sunnydale was one of the strongest mystical convergences on earth: There was a hellmouth there, and it drew an enormous, seemingly endless, number of vampires, demons, and assorted other nasties, all itching for a fight with a Slayer.

So Buffy's last chance for a normal life was taken from her, and she did not let go of it without a fight.

It followed, then, that she was probably itching for a fight the first time she and he actually met.

She'd been walking to the Bronze, and he had been following her.

He had a feeling she knew he was there when she turned abruptly into an alley. He trailed after, only to find the alley deserted.

He was honestly ambushed when she dropped down from a handstand on an overhead pipe about ten feet above his head. She bodyslammed him, and though he was on his feet quickly, she grabbed him and threw him up against the wall. Only when he put up his hands did she leave off her original plan of beating him to a pulp.

"Is there a problem, ma'am?" he'd drawled. He'd been faintly amused, and he saw that she saw it.

He also watched her give him a surreptitious once-over; he could tell she liked what she saw.

Nevertheless, she was all Slayer when she shot back, "There's a problem. Why are you following me?"

"I know what you're thinking," he began. She thought he was a vampire. Well, he *was* a vampire. But he couldn't tell her that on peril of his life.

"But don't worry," he continued. "I don't bite." There. That was the truth without all the fancy trimmings . . . and complicated explanations.

She backed off, a bit perplexed.

He decided to tease her a little, let out a bit of line and see if he could reel her in.

"Truth is," he said, "I thought you'd be taller. Or bigger. Muscles and all that. You're pretty spry, though."

She kept to the subject, and that impressed him even more.

"What do you want?"

"Same thing you do," he'd answered.

"Okay, what do I want?"

He had said, very seriously, "To kill 'em. To kill 'em all."

That was such a simple answer, though. Did he want to kill his own sire, Darla, when she threatened Buffy? To stake her in the back, see her turn in shock, and utter his name before she exploded into dust?

Did he want to kill Drusilla, whom he had driven insane? When she and Spike arrived in Sunnydale, he had told her to go away. He had not tried to kill her. He'd even hid her presence from Buffy.

And when it turned out that what both of them wanted, in addition to the deathdealing and the staking and the beheadings, was each other—how simple was that?

Now he stood and looked at the slip of paper in his Los Angeles apartment. He couldn't stand by now, just as he hadn't been able to stand by when Buffy was called.

Damn it.

As soon as it was dark, Angel got into his car and navigated his way down the 10 to Santa Monica. The permanent carnival on the pier was illuminated, the Ferris wheel turned merrily, and the lights cast a sheen on the ocean.

At the red light the Hilton was on his left; he saw a young couple sitting in an SUV in the valet circle. JUST MARRIED was painted in soap on the side of the vehicle.

The couple got out. They were dressed in casual but expensive clothes—linen, cotton, silk—and the woman, a leggy blonde, had on a hat.

She looked up at the young man—her husband—and reached on tiptoe to kiss him, facing Angel. Then her gaze slid past to Angel, and her eyes locked with his.

He looked away, unwilling to disturb their privacy. The light changed. He drove on.

The young woman was still looking at him.

It's not going to last, he found himself thinking.

Then there it was: the Coffee Spot. It was upscale, a nice place. That pleased him. Whoever Tina was, at least she wasn't slinging hash in a rundown diner.

He went inside. It was more properly a coffeehouse, not a coffee shop. The employees wore black pants and white shirts and the clientele was sophisticated. Soccer moms. Yuppies.

Angel got a coffee and surveyed the scene, standing to one side. A man—possibly the manager, judging from his air of authority—was talking to a striking girl with shoulder-length blond hair. The girl looked frustrated, the manager mildly contrite.

"Tina," he said, "I gotta do it by seniority. Everyone wants to work extra hours."

"I know. I just need . . ." She tried another tack.

"I'm good for Saturday nights, if other people want to go out. I'll double shift, whatever."

"You're on the list. Okay?" He was managing her. She knew it. "Thanks," she said, deflated.

She grabbed a cleaning rag and headed in Angel's general direction. He stepped forward, as if he might say something to her.

But when she glanced at him, he couldn't think of anything to say. *I'm rusty. I'm used to being alone.*

He looked away and sipped his coffee. She moved on, cleaning a service area a distance away.

Then he spotted a guy with a cute and friendly dog. A couple of young women who'd been passing by slowed to pet and coo over the dog.

Tina was heading back toward the counter. Angel seized the moment, edging toward the dog, holding out his hand to pet him.

"Sure is a cute little . . ." he began.

Tina, moving past him, didn't hear his opening gambit. Meanwhile, the cute and friendly dog backed away from Angel and lay down, cowed.

". . . doggie," Angel finished awkwardly. He felt incredibly conspicuous.

Oblivious, Tina began clearing the table next to her.

Angel screwed up his nerve and tried again.

"Do you, uh, how late are you open?"

She was startled. She looked up at him and asked, "Are you talking to me?"

As she did so, she inadvertently knocked a full mug of coffee off the edge of the table.

"Oh!" she cried.

Angel caught the full cup halfway to the floor and handed it back to her.

"Wow." She was impressed. "Good reflexes."

Without speaking, Angel nodded. *Man, I'm bad at this,* he thought.

She said, "Well, thanks. These come out of my paycheck."

"So," he began, "are you . . . happy?"

Good one.

Moron.

"What?" She was obviously confused, as well she should be. But it was too late to turn back now.

"You looked sort of . . . down."

Now she was edgy. "You been watching me?"

"No. I just, I was looking toward there . . ." He gestured. "And you walked through there. . . ."

Her smile was genuine. Her amusement, more so. "You don't hit on girls very often, do you?"

"It's been a while," he confessed. "I'm sort of new in town."

Her smile fell. "Do yourself a favor. Don't stay." She started to leave.

Angel said, "You never answered my question."

"Am I happy?" She looked at him. "You got three hours?"

Bingo.

"Do I look busy?"

She paused, considered. "I get off at ten."

Ten finally came. Angel leaned against his car as Tina showed. She had a nice dress on and a large carry bag was slung over her shoulder. She walked with purpose toward him.

"I suddenly feel underdressed," he said, feeling somewhat more in control. The old ways were coming back to him. Socializing, riding a bicycle.

Maybe.

He continued, "Did you want to get a drink, or—"

She held up her key ring, menacing him with a tube of Mace. "I know who you are, what you're doing here. You stay the hell away from me, and you tell Russell to *leave me alone.*"

The Mace wouldn't do permanent damage, but it would hurt. Besides, he had a mission. He told her, "I don't know anyone named Russell."

She didn't let her guard down for a millisecond. "You're lying."

He said earnestly, "No, I'm not."

"Then why were you in there watching me?"

"Because you looked lonely." He paused. "And I figured, then we have something in common."

She looked at him for a long moment, then lowered her Mace. Clearly, his words had hit home.

"I'm sorry," she said. "I'm really . . ."

"It's okay." His voice was soothing. He meant it. It was okay.

"No, it's not. . . ." She trailed off. "I'm sort of having 'relationship issues.' You probably guessed that."

Enter Batman, he thought. *Or am I Della Reese?*

But that felt very cynical. This girl was terrified. She needed a superhero.

Or at least a friend.

"Who's Russell?" he asked.

She shook her head.

He pressed just a little. "I'd like to help."

"Only help I need is a ticket home, and that wasn't me asking for money. I've taken . . . money before." That was a humiliation, and he knew it. "Never comes free."

"Where's home?"

"Missoula, Montana. Lots of open land, lots of drunk cowboys." The homesickness in her voice came through loud and clear. "Came here to be a famous movie star, but, um, they weren't hiring. Met a lot of colorful people on the way, though, which is why I come armed."

He looked at her squarely. "Fair enough."

She said, "You kind of remind me of the boys back home. Except you're not drunk."

Deadpan, he said, "I'm high on life."

"Yeah, it's a kick." She smiled at him, checked her watch. "Well . . . I gotta go to a fabulous Hollywood party." She pointed at her outfit. "Hence the glamour. Girl giving it owes me my security deposit."

She hesitated, as if she wasn't sure what else to say. Finally she came up with a pretty good closer.

"Well, it was nice threatening you."

Oh, no, you don't.

"You need a lift?"

She thought a moment. Then she took a step toward him.

"What's your name?" she asked.

"Angel."

He felt as if he'd told her a lot more than that.

It was a classy high-rise apartment building, the kind of good address that went for a lot of money in Los Angeles. People who couldn't afford to live in places like this often paid mail-drop companies to provide them with the right numbers and street names for their business cards and junk mail, so they could pretend to the world that they'd made it. It worked often enough.

They pulled into the underground parking lot, which was well-secured. Then they got into an elevator that took them straight up.

Tina led the way. When the door opened, a video

camera was pointed straight at them. The woman who held it was Tina plus five years of hard living. With her slightly curled brown hair, her delicate brows, and her slender neck, she reminded Angel— uncomfortably—of Jenny Calendar, whose slender neck he had broken two years ago.

Jenny had been the computer science teacher at Sunnydale High. More significantly, she had also been a technopagan who had begun assisting Giles in various battles against the forces of darkness— especially those on the Internet.

They had fallen in love, but that love was strained when a demon which Giles had called up as a young man possessed her. That time Angel had saved her life, forcing the demon to enter him instead. But Angel had taken her life. And as the camera stared at him like a baleful eye, it all came rushing back:

He had been lost then, his soul torn away from him yet again. Jenny, who besides being a techno-pagan, was a spy sent by her Gypsy clan, the Kalderash, to watch him. To make sure he suffered for crimes he had committed against her people.

For if he experienced even a moment of true happiness, his soul would be wrenched from his body once more, and he would revert to the pure state of demonic vampire.

And it had happened: He had found that happiness—in the arms of Buffy, on the night of her seventeenth birthday. They had given themselves to each other after Angel had put a Claddagh ring on her finger. It was the closest thing to a wedding and a honeymoon they had ever had.

But after the bliss, the Kalderash curse was reversed. One of the most brutal vampires ever created—Angelus, the One with the Angelic Face—was loosed upon the world.

Jenny had tried to restore his soul. She would have succeeded, too, the night he had come calling.

Sunnydale, 1998

Like any good computer person, Jenny Calendar was lost to the rest of the world as she continued working on translating the annals for the Rituals of the Undead. As she sat in her classroom and tapped on the keyboard, she talked to the screen.

"Come on, come on," she murmured.

The glow from the screen crossed over her face. She stared at the monitor for a few moments, and then she laughed.

"That's it! It's going to work. This will work."

She hit another key, rolled on her chair over to the old-fashioned tractor-feed printer, and watched the characters printing.

Then she raised her line of sight just slightly and jumped up in sheer fright.

Angelus, sitting at a desk with a smile on his face, had been watching her for at least ten minutes.

"Angel." She struggled not to show her panic as she slowly backed away. "How did you get in here?"

"I was invited," he said innocently, shrugging as if it were obvious. "The sign in front of the school? *'Formatia trans sicere educatorum.'* "

Jenny said breathlessly, " 'Enter, all ye who seek knowledge.' "

He chuckled and got to his feet. "What can I say? I'm a knowledge seeker." Holding out his hands, he started walking toward her.

"Angel," she blurted, terrified, "I've got good news."

"I heard." He sounded as if he were speaking to a child. "You went shopping at the local boogedy-boogedy store."

The glow on her desk attracted him. He picked up the crystal sphere and his voice dropped. "The orb of Thesulah. If memory serves, this is supposed to summon a person's soul from the ether, store it until it can be transferred."

He held it up. "You know what I hate most about these things?" he asked pleasantly. Then he hurled it against the blackboard, dangerously close to her head. Jenny ducked and screamed as it shattered around her.

He laughed. "They're so damned fragile. Must be that shoddy Gypsy craftsmanship, huh?"

He turned his attention to her computer. "I never cease to be amazed how much the world has changed in just two and a half centuries."

She was backing away, like he wouldn't notice. His good hearing picked up the rattle of the doorknob. But he knew the door was locked.

"It's a miracle to me," he went on, wide-eyed. "You put the secret to restoring my soul in here . . ." Savagely, he flung the computer to the floor. The monitor smashed against the linoleum and burst into flames. ". . . and it comes out here." He ripped the printout off the printer. "The Ritual of Restoration. Wow." He chuckled. "This brings back memories."

He tore it in half.

Her eyes widened. "Wait! That's your—"

"Oh. My 'cure'?" He grimaced an apology as he kept ripping. "No, thanks. Been there, done that. And déjà vu just isn't what it used to be.

"Well, isn't this my lucky day." He held the pages over the burning monitor. "The computer *and* the pages." He set them on fire and dropped them. Then he made a show of warming his hands. He crouched low. "Looks like I get to kill two birds with one stone."

She started edging toward the next door. But then

he turned to her, in full vamp face, and drawled, "And teacher makes three."

She tried to make a run for the door. He sprang up and caught her easily, and she screamed. With the supernatural strength of his kind, he flung her toward the wall. She hit the door, and the force of the impact pushed it open.

Slowly he advanced. Her forehead bleeding, she got to her feet, panting with terror, and flew down the corridor.

"Oh, good," Angelus said dangerously. "I need to work up an appetite first."

She raced for her life. Her heels clattered as she reached the first set of swinging doors in the corridor. Then she ran to the right, past the lockers and to the exit.

The door was locked.

She doubled back and saw his shadow looming through the panels of glass in the double doors. She took another exit. Down the breezeway she ran, arms pumping, looking back to see him shortening the distance between them. Light and shadow played on his monstrous features.

Like a quarry run to ground, she was forced to another entrance into the school. For a few thrilling moments, Angelus thought that door was locked too, but it finally gave way under her frantic pushes.

She lost time, and he was practically on top of her by the time she got the door open. He growled like an animal, anticipating the kill. She slammed the door in his face and ran on.

The bright overhead fluorescents cast a cold blue glow over the two of them as she lost more ground. Then she pushed the janitor's cleaning cart at him. It crashed into him and he stumbled over it, landing hard on the floor.

While he was down, she took the nearby flight of stairs. Gasping for breath, she looked over her shoulder as she darted past a semicircular window—street lamps and passing cars, the unsuspecting and uncaring normal world of urban night—and ran right into him.

She could move fast.

But he could move faster.

Her eyes widened as he put his chilled fingers to her lips, urging her to silence. His laughter was inhuman. She couldn't speak. Couldn't blink. Couldn't breathe.

"Sorry, Jenny. This is where you get off," he said in a low, gentle voice. And then he grabbed her head and twisted.

Her neck made an interesting crack.

Her lovely body tumbled to the floor.

A little winded, Angelus took a couple of deep breaths, and then he cocked his head.

"I never get tired of doing that."

Without another glance at the dead woman, he moved on.

"Smile for the camera," the woman at the party commanded. She added appreciatively, "Who's this hunk of tall, dark, and handsome?"

"He's a friend," Tina said. "Margo, I really need to talk to you."

Margo said offhandedly, "Get yourself a drink. I'll be there."

She turned the camera on other arriving guests. Tina and Angel drifted toward the hors d'oeuvres table. The apartment was elegant, with a great city view. It was packed with the young and the hip, everybody very on, making their moves while trying not to appear too eager.

Tina indicated the mountain of party sandwiches cut into star shapes.

"Cute," she said. "Everyone's a star."

Angel cut to the chase. "Who's Russell?"

She looked scared. "You don't want to know."

"Actually, I do."

She replied, "He's someone I made the mistake of trusting."

Margo sailed up to them and announced, "Here I am."

Tina said to Angel, "This won't take long."

Margo smiled fetchingly at the vampire. "I wouldn't leave that one unattended," she drawled.

The two women moved off. Angel looked around at the trendy crowd chatting and drinking. His awkwardness returned full force. He felt out of place, and that made him feel a little tired. Doyle probably didn't know what he had asked of Angel.

How much he had asked of Angel.

Then he found himself confronted by a tidy businessman-type guy. The man was about forty-five, and he stared at Angel intently.

He said, "You are a beautiful, beautiful man."

Angel was nonplussed. "Uh, thanks."

"You're an actor," the man continued.

"No."

The man held out a business card. "It wasn't a question. I'm Oliver; ask anyone about Oliver. They'll tell you that I am a fierce animal. I'm your manager as soon as you call."

Angel insisted, "I'm not an actor."

Oliver smiled. "Funny. I like the humor—I like the whole thing. Spelling has a pilot going up. I don't know what it's about, but you're perfect. Call me. This is not a come-on; I'm in a very serious relationship with a landscape architect."

Oliver, fierce animal that he was, swept away. Angel had no idea what to say. He left the card on the table and turned to look around some more.

Then he heard a familiar laugh.

A very familiar laugh.

Curious, he rounded a corner. And there she was, talking to a couple of men in suits: Cordelia Chase. Queen C.

How to describe Cordelia? The most self-absorbed, bravest, deeply narcissistic girl in Sunnydale? Cordelia had grown up pampered and wealthy, and as such, perhaps, had learned there were generally minor consequences for saying exactly what was on her mind. "Tact is just not saying stuff that's true," she had been fond of saying. "I'll pass."

A stunning girl-woman with dark hair and large deepset eyes, a slightly angular face, and full lips— Cordelia had been the bane of Buffy's life in Sunnydale, beginning with the very first day of school. She'd befriended Buffy, then never quite forgiven the Slayer for throwing in her lot with Xander Harris and Willow Rosenberg. The two had been social outcasts, but more loyal friends could not be found by anyone. Both had blossomed from knowing Buffy and fighting alongside her; Willow had even discovered a talent for spellcasting.

But Cordelia? Had she actually changed, as the others had? Angel was never certain. It seemed she had, for a time, due to the extreme sacrifice (for her) of status when she publicly dated Xander. But then she'd caught him kissing Willow, and she had reverted to type.

When she'd first met Angel, she had been attracted to him, and didn't hide that fact. Even when she knew his true nature. But they weren't in Sunnydale anymore. It was strange to see her out of habitat.

Would they be different with each other?

"Oh, Calloway is a pig!" she was saying to the group around her. "I won't even read for him anymore. How do you think Carrie got the part? Oh, *please.*" She did that thing with her eyes. "There's a short walk between acting and faking. Anyway, she's way too old. It should be someone fresh, you know, like a young Natalie Portman."

Angel said, "Cordelia."

She looked over at him, did a double take.

"Oh, my God! Angel!"

Her audience began to drift away as she went to Angel. She glanced anxiously at their retreat, torn, but somehow Angel won the coin toss.

"I didn't know you were in L.A. Are you living here?"

"Yeah. You?"

She preened a little. "Malibu. Little condo on the beach. It's not a private beach, but I'm young, so I forbear."

He was pleased for her. "And you're acting?"

"Can you believe it?" She did that thing with her hair. "I just started it as a way to make some quick cash and then—*boom!* It's my life. Lots of work. I'm just trying to keep grounded, not let it go to my head. So are you still"—she made claws and fangs—"grrrr?"

"Yeah." He shrugged. "There's not actually a cure for that."

"Right," she said brightly. "But you're not evil. You're not here to . . . you know, bite people. . . ."

He didn't blame her for checking. Their past did contain a significant Jekyll-Hyde quotient.

"Just gave a friend a ride," he assured her.

"Good." She was all white teeth and bright eyes. "Isn't this a great party?"

"Fabulous," he concurred, meaning, *Not really*.

She didn't catch it, didn't hear it. "So, who do you know?" she pressed. Then, off his look, she tried again. "Who do you know here? Somebody?"

"Just Tina. This isn't exactly my scene."

"Well, yeah, you're the only vampire here."

Angel couldn't help it. "I kind of doubt that."

She didn't catch that, either. *Same old Cordy.*

"Well, I better get mingly; I really should be talking to the people who are somebody," she said brightly. "But it was fun!"

She sailed off.

Tina was on her way back, looking none too

happy. Then she was intercepted by a tough-looking guy—harsh features, heavy brows—in a well-cut suit.

One thing about being a vampire for so long, Angel thought. *I've had some great outfits in my day.*

The guy—frankly, he looked like a thug—exchanged a few words with Tina. She was obviously not happy about that either. Then he put his hand on her arm, and she wrenched it away.

She moved to Angel and said, flustered, "Of course she doesn't have the money yet. Can we get out of here?"

Angel looked over at suit guy. "Who's that?"

"Just a creep. Can we please go?"

Angel complied. They headed for the door.

Stacey watched them go. Then he whipped out his cell phone.

She hadn't wrinkled his suit.

One point in her favor. But just one.

Tina tried to breathe. She had taken to holding her breath a lot lately, or else she took too many breaths, too shallow to do much good.

She had no idea how she had gotten herself into this mess. *A baby step at a time,* she told herself. *First you do one thing that feels a little off, and then another, and pretty soon you're knee-deep.*

Then you realize you've just spent the last six months of your life wading in quicksand.

She glanced up at Angel. His profile was already etched in her mind. His eyes were so dark you could just fall right into them. He was the kind of guy one might see for two seconds, but one would never forget any detail. That dark hair, the way he carried himself. Like a fighter who knew he could take on anybody, yet very wary.

There was something about him, a presence, a different-ness. It was clear he had his own demons. He wasn't comfortable in his skin. But an aura of power clung to him.

Who was he, anyway? Was he handing her a rope to pull her out, just so he could hang her?

Montana had never seemed so far away. Sometimes it was almost as if it had stopped existing. Or like home was something she made up to make herself feel better about her life.

What I wouldn't give for a drunk cowboy, she thought, and almost smiled.

She didn't even want to think about having someone like Angel in her life. *Really* in her life. The way she felt, that was aiming way too high.

The elevator doors slid open, and she and Angel stepped out into the parking garage.

By the time they both registered the presence of the three mean-looking guys, it was too late.

Two of them grabbed Angel and hustled him back into the elevator. The doors snapped shut.

Tina faced the third guy. She knew him. Knew who had sent him.

There were two elevators. The doors to the second one opened, and of course, Stacey was there.

Why did I think I was going to get out of this? she thought miserably.

Stacey said, "He just wants to see you, that's all."

Defeat. "Okay. No problem."

He indicated a waiting BMW 750. Tina's heart pounded as she obediently headed for it. Her hands were ice cold.

She bolted as soon as she could.

Her shoes clattered as she raced away. She could hear them behind her, gaining ground. She dodged between some parked cars.

And then they got her.

Hands grabbed her from behind and held her as she struggled. It was the guy who had blocked her way after they got Angel back in the elevator.

"Let go of me!" she cried, flailing. *"Let go of me!"*

They threw her in the car.

And she knew, right then, right there, that she was going to die.

ACT TWO

In the parking garage the BMW was revving. The guy who had tackled Tina was at the wheel. Tina was in back with the "creep."

The elevator doors opened and Angel leaped out, assessing the situation as quickly as he could.

His two attackers were on the floor, most definitely taken out of play. Not a big challenge, but they had slowed him down just enough, it appeared.

As Angel watched, the Beemer roared away.

Without hesitation Angel took off running in the opposite direction. He could guess the layout of the garage and he knew they would have to loop around to get out of the structure.

Desperate to cut his time, he jumped up on a parked car and ran across several more. He could hear the Beemer's engine above the heavy thuds of his boots. Or maybe that was his heart—which never beat.

He forced himself not to think about stumbling or falling or doing anything that would lose time. As high as he could, he leaped over the last car and landed precisely in the front seat—*go, Speed Racer!*—of the convertible . . .

. . . that was not his.

His car was nearby, but it was not this one. Not this one whose driver, as any driver in Los Angeles, had taken his keys with him.

"Damn," Angel gritted.

No time for anything else: He scrambled out and scrambled for his own vehicle like a pilot into his Harrier during a scramble.

The BMW screeched around a corner, with a clear shot for the exit.

By then Angel had gotten into his car and started it. Now he put the pedal to the metal and headed straight for the Beemer.

The Beemer's driver kept coming. Angel didn't slow, didn't turn, didn't flinch.

It looked as if it was going to be a brutal game of chicken.

Angel was okay with that.

The engines raced; both of them were going flat out; it was like some kind of Road Warrior joust to the death. Angel didn't know if he would survive, but it was more likely he would than the other guy. Still, whatever it took . . .

As fast as it took . . .

Their front bumpers were just about to crush; at the last minute the other guy yanked the wheel.

The BMW swerved into the concrete wall and ground to a halt in a shower of sparks and scrunching metal. Angel figured the only thing that kept it from flattening like a pancake was that world-renowned German engineering.

Angel was already there by the time the driver got out and pulled a gun. Angel kicked it out of his hand. It went straight up in the air. The thug looked up to watch it; Angel smashed him in the face, grabbed the gun out of the air, and shoved it in the neck of the other guy—Tina's unwanted party companion—as he barreled out of the backseat. Tina was getting out, too.

Her seat mate said, "I don't know who you are, but you don't want to get involved here, trust me."

Angel pretty much ignored him. He said, "Tina, get in the car."

She did.

The other guy looked at him with contempt. "You know what?" he taunted. "I don't think you're gonna pull that trigger."

Without missing a beat, Angel punched him in the face. The guy was on the ground in an instant.

"Good call," Angel said.

He climbed into his car. The guy on the ground was practically gnashing his teeth as he stared balefully at Angel.

"Nice party, huh?" Tina said.

Angel replied, "Little too fabulous for me."

He slammed the car into gear and roared away. He was furious, perhaps all the more so because he could still remember a time when he was the one who terrified vulnerable women like this. In fact, he turned them into monsters. And those monsters made more monsters.

And those monsters killed lots of people.

One had only to look at his demonic children, Dru and her paramour, Spike, to see how culpable he was.

Dublin, 1838

It was Christmas, and the snow lay deep and crisp and even. It covered the street; people and carriages milled about, shopping and smiling, in high anticipation of feasting and revelry. Carolers sang and orphans begged. For once, their chilblain fingers touched coin: After all, 'twas the season.

And he came, himself in his high hat and furtive looks. Daniel, his name was, and he was a craven and a cheat. He owed Angelus money, quite a lot of it, and he had continued to play on markers which proved to be of no value. Worse, Angelus had learned, he had pawned his prized family heirlooms and now had no real means to speak of.

Daniel had tried to avoid him for weeks, growing more nervous with the passage of time, and Angelus had allowed him to imagine he was dodging him successfully. It was amusing to watch the lad degenerate, vastly pleasing to observe the progressive fraying of his nerves.

Of course, that might also have something to do with Daniel's upcoming wedding, to the daughter of a family who expected their darling girl to be gracefully provided for. One word of his impoverished condition, and Daniel's fiancée would be taken away from him in the twinkling of a diamond.

But for Angelus, the game was growing dull. Still, from that Christmas Eve on, Angelus was never quite certain what moved him to kill Daniel that particular night.

Not that it ever bothered him. It was simply . . . intriguing.

Daniel had begged for his life, reminded Angelus about his fiancée, tried to renegotiate the loan. Angelus had allowed the man a wee bit o' hope, and then he had enjoyed his own Christmas revels.

Lovely in a beautiful white fur cape and an enchanting hood and muff, Darla had stood in the snow, no breath emanating from her blood-red lips.

Her eyes glittered like ice. As Angelus spattered blood on the clean, white snow, she watched from the crested shadows, beaming at Angelus.

"Bravo, dear one," she had said, in her honey-warm voice.

"So you approve?" he queried, wiping his mouth with the back of his hand.

"Of course." She smiled sweetly at him.

She approved of everything Angelus did.

In those days, at least.

London, 1860

But even the closest of lovers require a holiday after a century together. No matter the closeness, the intimacy, the joy: One simply must have a moment to gather oneself back together.

Their parting was amiable, and they promised to return to each other within a decade.

At first Angelus sorely missed Darla. She was his sire and, frankly, the only vampire he knew well enough to trust slightly more than he mistrusted her. He found himself thinking, *I'll have to tell her about this*, after every grand adventure.

Thus the need to carefully record every detail of his nights became a habit; and he realized he was able, in this way, to more fully experience what was happening at the moment it actually occurred. This lent spice to his life, which was previously missing.

And so he stayed away for a longer time than he would have planned. Fifteen years, then sixteen.

Then twenty.

It may be true that absence makes the heart grow fonder.

But that is if one still has a heart.

Angelus, being of the undead, officially possessed such an organ, but it no longer beat.

Into the twenty-fifth year he found himself missing Darla less and less. It was in that time that he truly began living for himself. He traveled widely and developed quite a reputation among the forces of darkness. He was universally feared. No one wanted to cross Angelus, the Scourge of Europe. It was exhilarating, to say the least.

Finally he made it to London, the city of his youthful dreams, and it was even more astonishing than he had imagined. Of course, the entire world was more astonishing than when he had been alive. A century had gone by, and so very much had happened: steam engines, electricity, the telegraph. And so many other wonders were on the way.

But nothing compared to the ancient wonder of the hunt. The primeval joy of the kill.

The eternal celebration of evil.

As in this particular moment, when Angelus had entered the confessional of a small Whitechapel church, ripped open the throat of a Catholic priest, and killed him.

He was sitting with the man's body still warm in his grasp when he realized that someone had entered the penitent's side of the box.

A shaky girl's voice announced that it had been an entire two days since her last confession.

And his unbeating, dead heart was won. Posing as the priest, he urged her to confide in him. Trust in him.

She told him that she saw visions. She had seen that morning's mine accident before it had occurred. Her mother insisted that foreseeing the future belonged to the provenance of the Almighty himself. A mere wretch of a girl should not be able to do such things . . . unless she were cursed by the Devil himself.

Oddly moved and highly amused, he assured her that this was indeed so. She was a hellspawn, and therefore, she should yield to evil. Fulfill God's plan by performing vile deeds. The poor chit was bewildered, but she was a good girl at heart, and good girls listened to their priests.

So she kept coming back for more of his terrible advice. Her name, he learned, was Drusilla.

As he had with his own family, he murdered all her relatives. He tore out the throats of her friends and of a boy she had hoped to marry.

Anyone she spoke of to her confessor behind the rood died soon after. Convinced of her inherent wickedness, she fled to a convent, and for a time he let her soak up the purity of the good sisters around her.

Then, on the day she was to take the veil, he changed her as Darla had changed him.

That was what drove her completely and irreversibly mad.

Now they two ran together, and on occasion Darla joined them. Dru changed a young Brit named William the Bloody, and they were a pack. A fearsome clan of the most brutal vampires in history.

Angelus led them in savagery and mercilessness. He inspired them to torture and torment their victims. William became "Spike," for his habit of driving railroad spikes into his victims.

Drusilla discovered she had a wonderful gift for mesmerizing her victims. She was like a cobra, coiling to strike, holding the gaze of her prey as it shuddered and trembled. It was glorious to behold.

It was highly satisfying to Angelus that she was his get. With a native skill far exceeding Darla's, he had made a marvelously base creature.

Drusilla was his most glorious achievement, and he took partial credit, at least, for most of her particularly sadistic deeds.

London, 1883

Drusilla stood watching, her eyes shining, as her Angelus dallied with Margaret, a pretty young servant. Drusilla herself wore a fine frock of brilliant red velvet, and she had garnets around her neck. There were Christmas roses and pearls in her hair, and Angelus was formal and handsome and exquisite in his evening clothes.

The young servant—stupid cow—was uneasy with the attentions of her employer's guest. How could a woman, mortal or vampire, resist the kisses and caresses of Angelus, the One with the Angelic Face? The Scourge of Europe, the Terror of Mongolia—

—Drusilla's sire, and her dearest love?

"Spike, look," she whispered, and Spike drifted to her side. He was fidgeting with his dress clothes; a Cockney, as she was, he was still unused to bucking the class system. No matter; he was her other dearest love, and *she* had sired *him*.

"Spike, it's grand watching him, isn't it?" she cooed. "He's so masterful. Such a romantic."

He grunted. "He always does this," he complained. "Goes for the frisson. I say, slap her around, show her your teeth, and get on with it. At the very least he should torture her a little. But it's always this . . . this minuet he's dancing."

"It's a matter of elegance," Drusilla insisted. "He has it. He's more upper class than us, you know."

"Humph. He's Irish." Spike made a face. "Any English beggar's better than an Irish king."

"Have a care," she said delightedly. "He'll rip out your throat if he hears you."

"Let him try." Spike touched her cheek. "I wish he would. I'd kill him, and then I'd have you all to meself."

"Or so you assume." She glittered at him, dimpling, giggling. She adored them both, her two strong men. It made her feel like a duchess when they challenged each other for her company. Always in jest . . . or so they liked her to think. But they were like any other two boys: playing at roughhousing, but each with a knife behind his back in the event things got out of hand.

Meanwhile, the maidservant was begging to be allowed to return to the party, and Angelus was blocking her way. She was truly becoming very afraid. Drusilla could smell her fear. She could hear the woman's heart pumping all the nice, warm blood.

"It's delicious," Drusilla murmured.

"Speaking of delicious, by the time he's done, there'll be nothing decent in the whole house left to drink," Spike groused. "Did you have that punch? What was in it, sugar water and milk? The champagne's already all gone."

"You should have joined the men for brandies after supper. Angelus did," she added pointedly.

"*You* said you were hungry," he grumbled.

"So I did." She preened. She'd sent him on a fool's errand; he'd gone off and nabbed a young girl selling chestnuts on the corner. Meanwhile, she and Angelus had shared a few private, tender moments alone on the terrace. Such was the nature of their little family.

She had only nibbled at the girl, and Spike had been pouting ever since, going on so about all the trouble he'd gone to to provide her a decent meal. *Cor*, he was as bad as a fishwife.

"Besides," she added prissily, "you take far too much strong drink. You didn't drink half that much before I changed you." She ran her nails down the side of his face. "Aren't you happy, luv? Don't you know I love you best? It's only that he's my sire."

"I don't believe you for a minute," he hissed at her, but she could see the hope in his eyes. She loved his weakness.

Slowly she turned and whispered, "I'll make it up to you, Spike. Don't I always?" Her eyes widened. "I hear sleigh bells. Or are those dead fairies and angels, begging Father Christmas to bring them back their souls?"

"It's the howling of Irish wolves," Angelus growled behind her.

"Angelus," she said delightedly.

His mouth was smeared with blood. Drusilla pulled a handkerchief from the bodice of her dress and set about wiping it away.

"Leave off with that," Spike said, irritated. To Angelus, he asked, "Where's the body?"

"Drained and tossed," Angelus replied casually.

"That's not very polite," Drusilla chided. "Spike's gone without to make me happy. And then I barely touched my meal." She smiled sweetly at Spike, who refused to smile back.

"My dinner has a son," Angelus drawled.

Drusilla clapped her hands. "Oh, a tender, fresh one," she said happily to Spike. "See? He came through for you after all. And you so grumpy." She cupped Spike's cheek. "It's Christmas, luv. Say Merry Christmas."

Spike glared at Angelus.

Angelus glared back.

"Merry bleedin' Christmas," Spike said between clenched teeth.

Drusilla was pleased. "That's the spirit."

Cordelia knew it was not a Malibu condo.

It wasn't even a condo.

It was a depressing, crummy apartment in a depressing, crummy apartment building.

The dress was gorgeous, though.

And Cordelia took very good care of it. She pressed it after every party and hung it up carefully in her threadbare closet.

She'd learned a lot about taking care of nice clothes, but not from when she could buy them without looking at the tags. It was after her parents lost all their money because they didn't bother giving any of it to the government.

So, no college tuition money, no prom dress money, even—Xander had paid for her prom dress, *of all people*—although if she could actually admit it to herself, it did seem like something he would do.

No money for anything, not even dreams.

Sitting in her slip on her little bed, she hit the Play button on her phone machine.

"You have one new message," her machine informed her.

She kept listening.

"Cordy, it's Joe at the agency. No luck again. I'm having trouble booking auditions. The networks are saying they've seen enough of you. Which means it's time to take a little breather, let 'em forget they remember ya . . . so don't call—you know, no need to call me. I'll buzz ya if something changes. 'Bye."

The machine added, "You have no more messages."

Cordelia sat for a long moment. Then she picked

up a napkin and unwrapped it, revealing two star-shaped sandwiches from the party. Dinner.

She lifted one to her mouth, took a bite, and chewed slowly.

Through her window the city looked dark. She couldn't remember ever feeling so hopeless. Okay, except for the time she and Buffy had been chained down in the basement of a frat house, and their reptile god, Machida, had tried to munch them for dinner.

Not to mention the time her supposedly dead boyfriend, Daryl, almost got his kid brother to cut off her head so she could be the centerpiece of his new patchwork girlfriend à la Dr. Frankenstein.

Or on Halloween, when everyone but she went a little insane (a little? a *lot!*) and Buffy became this disgustingly wimpy girl.

Kinda like Cordelia was being.

Resolutely she finished the sandwiches. Then she picked up her book titled *Actors and Auditions*.

As she dutifully read, her stomach growled with hunger.

"Stop that. How rude," Cordelia groused, near tears.

They were in Angel's apartment.

Tina came out of his bathroom in a T-shirt over her black work pants. She dropped her party dress in her large carryall.

"My Girl Scout training," she explained. "Be prepared. I can live out of this for days if I have to."

Girl Scout, Angel thought sadly. *She probably took ballet lessons and giggled about boys at slumber parties.*

A few lifetimes ago.

"Good," he said. " 'Cause you can't go back to your place. You can stay here."

"Yeah." She glanced at the bed. "I guess this is the part where you comfort me. Not like you didn't earn it."

She gave him a hard look, her emotions churning beneath the surface.

When he moved toward her, she tensed.

He said, "No. This is the part where you have a safe place to stay while we figure things out."

Her face betrayed her confusion. "You don't want to . . . ?"

"You've got enough people taking advantage of you right now."

Her eyes filled with tears. She tried to brush them away. "Boy, are you ever in the wrong town."

She sank onto the couch and cried. Angel gave her a tissue.

She said, "Thank you."

Gently he asked, "How about some tea?"

She nodded. He headed into the kitchen and started filling the pot.

"I'm just so tired," she said. "I can't sleep. He's going to find me." She sounded more defeated than anything. "Russell always finds you."

"Russell have a last name?"

"Yeah, but you don't need to know it," she said firmly. "You've done enough already. This is L.A. Guys like him get away with murder."

He had not forgotten that a demon who could channel some Powers that Be somewhere had given him Tina's name and workplace.

Maybe this is why.

"Who'd he murder?" he asked.

She took a moment.

"I don't know. Maybe nobody. He's got the bucks, likes to hang with starlets and such." She shrugged. "He was nice at first. I'm not an idiot. I know he's gonna want something in return—I figured what the hell, at least I'd be eating good."

Angel moved back to her. "What does he want in return?"

She was embarrassed. "He likes to . . . he likes pain. I mean he really does; he talks about it like it's a friend of his."

Angel took that in. He had known monsters like that.

He himself, for one.

"And you don't leave him," she continued. "He tells you when he's had enough. I knew a girl,

Shanise; she tried to get away. She disappeared off the face of the earth. He finds you."

"Not anymore," he told her. Promised her.

The teapot whistled, and Angel headed into the kitchen.

After less than half a cup, she dozed. Angel covered her with a blanket and studied her for a moment.

Then his gaze fell on her bag.

He put it on the table and reached inside.

The first thing he found was her address book. She'd written her name and address on the first page—usually not all that good an idea, if you were running with the kind of crowd she was.

He started thumbing through it. A business card fell out. He looked at it. WOLFRAM & HART, ATTORNEYS AT LAW.

Weird logo, he thought, laying the card aside.

He kept riffling through the book until he found what he was looking for.

Shanise Williams.

All the phone numbers beside her name were crossed out.

Written off, he thought.

In the early twentieth century Charlie Lummis, then head librarian at the Los Angeles Public Library, commissioned a branding iron, patterned after those used in Mexican and monastery libraries. Such irons were called *Marcas del Fuego*. Fire marks. Lummis used his to brand the covers of the library's more important books.

So it had to be mere irony that so many of the library's holdings were destroyed in a terrible fire in 1986. Those which could be replaced were, but the branding iron was never recovered from the huge piles of soaking ash and sodden pulp—the results of the efficient sprinkler system.

Now, late at night, the refurbished library was a dimly lit, deserted cavern. If any of Angel's haunts resembled the Batcave, this was the one.

He wondered when he'd see the Irish demon again. He didn't exactly doubt that he would. But it occurred to him that maybe this was a test of the new Los Angeles superhero defense system. If he didn't pull this off, maybe the Powers that Be would move on to another candidate for savior of Los Angeles. Maybe there was some other poor schmuck vampire with a soul who needed a hobby.

The computer screen lit up, casting his face in the glow of soft X rays. He'd called up a newspaper site on this particular monitor. Named it computer number three. He'd already booted up two other computers. He was gathering data from all three.

Call him the Man Who Fell to Earth.

On the news site keyboard, Angel typed in MUR-DERS, YOUNG WOMEN.

Meanwhile, on the second screen, information was coming up in response to Search: WILLIAMS, SHANISE.

It read, ACTRESS, MEMBER S.A.G., A.F.T.R.A.; DANCER IN LAS VEGAS UNDER THE NAMES LYLA WILLIAMS, LYLA JONES.

He typed WILLIAMS, LYLA, and JONES, LYLA, and hit Search.

Meanwhile, he shifted to the third screen and scrolled POLICE FILES.

Back on the first screen, he scanned various back-page headlines. *Unidentified Woman Found Strangled. . . . Hiker Finds Body in Angeles Crest Forest. . . . Murder Victim Trashed in Dumpster. . . .*

She had never made the front pages. Back page all the way, ashes to ashes, morgue to a Jane Doe deepfreeze pending closing of the case. After all, who was she? In the big drama that was Hollywood, nothing more than a background extra.

He sighed as he glanced over at the second screen. There she was: LYLA JONES, DANCER A.K.A. SHANISE WILLIAMS. Dressed up in a Vegas costume. She looked happy in the photograph. He doubted seriously that she had been at the time, if ever.

On screen three he scrolled through MISSING PER-

SONS REPORTS and JANE DOES. He stopped, thinking he'd caught something, and scrolled back.

It was a Jane Doe report: Five foot ten, 115 pounds—IDENTIFYING MARKS: tattoo on left shoulder.

On the second screen he went back to the Vegas photo of Lyla Jones.

She had a small flower tattoo on her left shoulder.

It was almost dawn by the time Angel slid his car into the covered parking by his building. The sun was heating up the last traces of night. He'd cut it pretty damn close.

Oh, well, other people skydive for thrills, he thought ironically.

It was strange how the sun pulled on him, made him tired. He had never understood precisely why. He hadn't made the time to investigate it. Figured it had something to do with being demonic, forces of darkness, yada yada yada. Whatever worked. And he didn't, in full sunlight.

As he was moving down the hall, he heard a woman shouting.

"No! Please don't! I can't."

Tina was still on the couch, in the throes of a nightmare. He crossed to her.

"I can't—" she cried.

"Tina," he said.

She screamed, arching up, clawing at his face, real horror in her eyes.

"No!" she shouted.

"It's all right," he urged. "Everything's all right."

She recognized him. Then she collapsed into his arms.

"He was here," she said brokenly.

He held her. "It's just a dream. It's okay now."

"Don't let me go," she pleaded.

She held on even tighter, rocking a little, touching his hair, his face. He struggled with the memories of the last time he had been touched . . . when he had held Buffy in his arms.

It had happened very long ago. In another world, in another place. Now he had to forget that moment.

He put his hand over hers, responding. And then he caught himself and gently pulled back.

He knew she was frightened, but he had to ask her about what he'd learned.

"Did your friend Shanise have a tattoo on her left shoulder?"

She nodded. "A daisy."

Damn. "I think she was murdered." There was no gentle way to say it. "And there've been others. He picks girls with no families, no one to care."

She looked at him, then away, very frightened.

"You don't have to be afraid," he told her. *You*

have someone who cares, he added silently. "You're safe here."

Still looking away, she said, "No."

"Yes," he insisted.

But he had lost her attention. Because she was looking at a crumpled slip of paper on the end table.

The one Doyle had given him: TINA, COFFEE SPOT, S.M.

"Why do you have that?" Her voice rose as she pulled away from him, standing. "You knew who I was when you walked in there last night!"

"No," he protested, "I didn't. I just . . . had your name." He was frustrated beyond words. "It's complicated."

She was terrified. "I'm sure. Big, complicated game Russell is working on my head. What's he paying you for?"

"He's not. You have to—"

"You're just like him!" She shoved him away and grabbed a lamp. "You stay away from me. I'm getting out of here."

He couldn't let her leave. It was a death sentence for her if she did.

"Let me—"

She hurled the lamp at his head and ran out the back door.

She ran for all she was worth, down the hall, past

Angel's car into the covered parking lot. Angel appeared, running after her.

"Tina!"

She kept going, leaving the covered lot, Angel right behind her. As she raced into the sunlight, he grabbed her arm.

"Please listen to—"

The sun hit his hand on her arm and it burst into flames. Rushes of pain ignited his body as Tina screamed, and he wrenched his hand back into the shadows, howling in pain.

In his extremity he morphed into his vampire visage. Tina's screams became bloodcurdling shrieks, and she ran as if for her life.

Angel collapsed against the building, cradling his hand, breathing hard, watching her go.

I'm going to lose my security deposit, Tina found herself thinking, in a strange mixture of everyday thinking shot through with blind panic. She was trying hard to make plans, stay focused, but all she could think about was how Russell's spy had turned into a monster before her eyes. *Was calling himself Angel some kind of a joke?*

She grabbed a small traveling bag and dumped it on the open sofa bed. *Always had that spring that stuck into my back; this place is a dump; oh, my God, he just changed into a—a demon or something. One minute he's this handsome guy and—*

She bent down and lifted up the thin mattress, took out her trusty .38. Back home, she'd blasted fruit cocktail cans with it. She had never dreamed in a million years she'd ever really *need* a gun.

She threw a few things in the bag.

Then she sensed a presence and spun, pointing the gun straight out.

At Russell.

There he was. The pain man. Mid-forties, charming, so incredibly well-dressed. His full lower lip curved in his signature smile, his hair slicked back. He looked so good, it was hard to believe he was the worst news on the planet.

"Tina. What are you doing?" he asked, his voice filled with concern. "Where have you been? I've been worried sick about you."

She kept the gun pointed at him. "What did you do to Shanise?"

He looked a little surprised. "Nothing."

Her voice shook. "I want the truth, Russell!"

"She wanted to go home," he said reasonably. "I bought her a ticket to Pensacola."

"No. She's dead."

His surprise turned into puzzlement. "What do you mean? She called me yesterday. She's trying to get back into school, wanted me to pull strings. Who's been telling you these things?"

She held her ground, but she was uncertain. She didn't know what to think.

"Look, we both know I live outside the box, but I don't go around killing my friends."

He moved toward her, getting very close. He seemed so kind, so concerned. She was even more confused.

"I've had everybody I know looking for you," he continued.

She just stared at him. She was frozen to the spot. Almost before she realized what he was doing, she let him take the gun.

But it was something of a relief. Maybe if he knew she trusted him . . . if she trusted him . . . he would be trustworthy.

"If you're sick of L.A., if you need rent . . . you know I only want to help you." He sounded so kind. He was so rich and powerful. He had said he would take care of her, and he would, wouldn't he?

"Just tell me what you want," he finished.

She said mournfully, "I want to go home."

"Done. Poor thing." She let him put his arms around her. "Who's been spinning your head like this?"

"I don't know. I thought you hired him," she confessed. "He turned into something. . . ."

He stroked her cheek and looked at her very kindly.

"It was the most horrible thing I've ever seen," she added, allowing herself to confide in him.

He said, "Well, you're young."

Then he turned into something that looked like the monster Angel had become—only much, much worse.

Everything fled out of her except pure horror. Her last gesture was to open her mouth. But she couldn't move her lips. She couldn't scream.

She could do nothing as the demon who had been the multimillionaire Russell Winters chomped down hard and vicious, and killed her.

SPIKE AND DRU

Somewhere in Hungary, 1956

When they arrived close to Halloween, Spike and Dru had had no way of knowing that their rustic little village was about to be invaded by the Soviet Union.

The loving couple were there because they'd heard a rumor that Angelus had been spotted, and Dru had insisted they look for him. She was always insisting they look for him. King Arthur's Knights of the Round Table hadn't looked for the bleeding Holy Grail with the zeal Dru looked for him.

She had not seen her sire in almost sixty years. No one had. She had no idea if he was alive or dead—speaking in vampire terms—but she had never ceased querying after him.

They'd been due to meet him in the Carpathians

in 1898, have a bit of a jaunt through the Old Country. Chew up some peasants and enjoy the local wine. But the bloke had never shown.

One year passed, then two, and Dru was fairly much preoccupied with what had happened to Angelus and nothing much else. Her anxiety was understandable, the big noise being her sire and all, but frankly, it got bloody boring. All her talk about the air whispering to her that he was not dead, nor of the living, blah blah. Something about his soul, which they all knew had been put out in a leaky boat when Darla had given him the gift.

After a time Spike learned to deal with it. Or so he assured her. He even helped her on this fool's errand. It became something of a hobby of sorts.

A week before, in Budapest, she had paid some minor chaos demon a handsome sum for the startling information that Angelus had been spotted in the Communist Bloc. With a bit more snooping about, some tarot readings, and a couple of visions, they'd settled on Hungary as his most likely hunting ground. So here they were, tally-ho, resuming the hunt.

Meanwhile the square just outside this little café—Minou—was filled with Soviet soldiers. An incredible number of them. The locals were awash in quaking fear and utter panic.

Spike feared a stampede.

"Dru, darling, she ain't coming, all right? Most likely she's been run over by one of those blasted tanks. I'd say it's high time we got out of here," Spike said, not for the first time that evening, and not for the fiftieth, since this meeting was arranged.

"She'll be here." Dru poked her fingernails through the green oilcloth covering on the table. "If she knows what's good for her." She gave him one of her come-hither looks. "Right?"

"Too right, Dru."

A coquette, she. There were times she melted him with her sweet little ways. She was his sire, and he owed her a lot for this great grand thing called being a vampire. He tried to remind himself of that when she went off her head about Angelus.

Hungary hadn't changed much in all the years Spike had been a vampire. It was still quite quaint and folksy, despite the fact that the Soviets had invaded it two years before. They were up to their eyeballs in hanged counterrevolutionaries, but everybody still wore embroidered vests and adorable short boots.

He knew Dru loved this kind of cultural thing. Her penchant for the gowns of her own lifetime blended in perfectly. She could swirl and dance to her heart's content in laces and velvets, and feel herself quite at home in the crush of the cattle.

Ah, the sweet cattle: It was incredibly easy to find

food; everyone was frightened and timid because of the big, bad Russians. All you had to do for a five-courser was to ask to see some papers, watch the poor bloke pale and fumble, and strike.

Two wineglasses sat on the table. Spike's was empty, and Drusilla's was untouched. She kept making little stabbing motions with her fingers and humming softly to herself. It helped to keep her calm, even if Spike did, upon occasion, ask her to stop. Not often, though. She didn't like him to ask her to stop.

He wasn't certain that she could, anyway. It had become a habit. Or a nervous tic. Or an extension of her loopiness.

"Dru, luv, can you hear that noise outside? That's the soldiers droning like bees in a honeycomb. Something's happening. This place is not safe."

What Drusilla had failed to tell Spike was that she loved the soldiers. All that heaving noise! She loved the dour, uniformed young Russians.

In fact, she loved them so much that she had had one for dinner earlier that evening, while Spike had been off arranging the rendezvous with the Gypsy woman who claimed to have seen Angelus.

Now she burped delicately and smiled across the table.

"Whoops," she said, fluttering her lashes a bit.

Now he reached across the table and took her hand. "You've got the longest fingers," he said. She made a jabbing motion. "Very strong, too."

"Would you like my wine?" she asked.

He looked tempted. He half-reached for it, then saw the pensive look on her face.

"What?" he asked petulantly, knowing she was all skitterish about if they were finally going to be re-united with himself.

She shook her head. "My Spike is in a bad mood," she observed. "I don't like it. It makes my head ache."

"Just nervous, poodle," he admitted freely. "Promise me that if the old bat comes up dry, we'll leave."

She was all smiles and cuddles. "We could go back to Spain."

He grinned at her. "The bulls."

She lowered her chin and peered seductively through her upper lashes. "The bulls."

"Brilliant." He reached for her glass and took a healthy swallow. "We can have your birthday party there."

She dimpled at him. "I'm reaching that age where a girl doesn't like to be reminded of her birthday."

"It's a mark of distinction for our kind," he observed. "The longer you live . . ." He touched his temple. "Brains is what makes you last. And a good upper cut." He grinned. "And heartlessness, of course."

"Grrrrrr." She made a slicing motion, as if to cut open his throat.

They smiled adoringly at each other.

Just then the front door opened, and a figure in a shapeless sort of dress appeared. A scarf completely covered her hair. The figure's features were sharp and its nose, hooked. The eyebrows were a steely gray, the eyes a steely black. It wore a five o'clock shadow, as they said in America.

"It's the Gypsy woman," Spike muttered. "We ain't been stood up after all."

"Are you sure?" Dru asked uncertainly, then added, "That she's a woman?"

"Looks can be deceiving, but I believe she's a female," Spike answered, knowing that he sounded mildly defensive.

The Gypsy looked at Dru and crossed herself. Dru flinched slightly at the insult, but she kept her composure.

After she made a few stabbing motions and thought she saw Spike's head shimmer with moonlight, that is.

The Gypsy shuffled toward them. She was holding something in her hand, and Dru and Spike recoiled as she drew near.

"Oh, crikey, she's got garlic," Spike groaned.

"Probably loaded down to the gills with crosses and holy water, Dru. Let's get out of here. This entire trip is not right."

Dru was frightened. She felt that, too—not right—but she couldn't walk away without knowing if the woman really did know about Angelus.

So she squared her shoulders and murmured, "Give me a chance with her. Please, Spike."

"You're risking both our lives."

"I owe it to him."

"Dru, pet, face it," he said anxiously. "All these years. Either he's dead, or he's abandoned—"

"No." Dru growled at him. "Down, bad dog!"

She rose out of her chair.

The Gypsy woman froze. She held out a cross and said, *"Upreiczi."*

"Isn't that Rumanian?" Spike asked suspiciously.

"I don't know." Dru felt fluttery. "Gypsies, they come from all over. I—"

The Gypsy shouted, and the door burst open. At least half a dozen soldiers burst into the room. They were followed by a mob of people, at least thirty, falling over themselves to get to Dru and Spike.

"Strigoiu!" someone shouted.

"I think *that's* Hungarian," Spike bellowed as he leaped from the table and tipped it on its side. He grabbed Dru's arm and began to drag her in the opposite direction.

"Spike!" she shrieked as her bootheel caught on the leg of their table. She shook it off as he inadvertently yanked on her arm, making her lose her balance.

She half-fell, half-slid forward on her opposite foot, crumpling into a sort of kneeling, and he dragged her up to her feet. He looked at her hard, yelling, "Come on, baby!" as the mob made for them.

Gunshots rang out.

Then Spike was pulling her along, shouting on about the world going mad. From what she could tell as they burst through the back door of the little café, the soldier she had had for dinner had been found. The Gypsy, on her way, had recognized the bite marks and informed the locals. And the Russian soldiers had thought it all some kind of rebellion and followed after to put it down.

It was actually a bit funny, or so she thought, giggling to herself as Spike led the way down the tiny, cobbled alleyways. He was all worked up over it, rather frantic, actually, and she wanted to tell him to mellow out, as they said these days.

"C'mon, c'mon," he ordered her, jerking hard as he slammed into yet another alley and looked up and down the street. Soft lights from windows illuminated their way.

"Spike, stay cool, *Daddy-o,*" she said, choking back laughter.

His eyes flashed. "Dru, this is bloody serious business. Will you please pay attention?"

She shrugged, still chuckling. She swept her arm in a gesture at the empty alleyway.

"We've lost them, Spike. We're safe and sound." She spun in a circle, her black and crimson embroidered skirts billowing. "I'm a bell. Ding, dong!"

"Oh, God, Dru. Most of the time I find your madness quite fetching. But at the moment . . ." He ran his hands through his long hair. "We won't be safe until we get out of this bleeding city. These people are at war. They're terrified of everything. They'd like nothing better than to kill something."

"Oh, pish posh, we're shadows." She flicked her fingers at him. "Boo. We're invisible."

Then, as if to put the lie to her words, they came.

From each end of the alley they came. Black berets and blousy shirts, soldiers in the drabbest of uniforms, eyes blazing; some had made it to the rooftops above Dru and Spike.

As Spike whirled in a circle, the ones on the roofs shouted to the others, running and pointing at the pair.

Then Dru did something very foolish: She changed.

Her vampire visage was clear for all to see.

Everyone froze. She growled at them, her golden eyes darting from the throng of attackers at one end of the street to the mob at the other end.

Then, as if on cue, both groups charged them.

Spike changed then, too, and rushed forward with a roar to take on the first man to reach him. He was tall and silver-haired, and he carried a wicked carving knife, which he lofted above his head.

Spike reached up and grabbed the man's upraised arm, still running toward him, and used the force of his momentum to dislocate his shoulder. Howling in pain, the man dropped the knife. Spike caught it handily and gutted him like a fish.

Then he used the body like a shield as two more men reached him, one of them an armed Soviet soldier, the other a local, and stabbed the soldier in the stomach. As the man shrieked and fell, the local tumbled over him, and all Spike needed to do to him was give him a good, swift kick in the temple.

He hazarded a glance at Dru and couldn't repress his grin of admiration. Somehow, she'd gotten herself two impressive-looking guns, one in each hand, and she fired them simultaneously. His girl, the six-shooter. Who was that American girl with all the brass? Annie Oakley.

As Dru found her rhythm, at least three people fell, one a fetching young girl, and six or seven of the brutish louts scrambled backward. Two of those hit the dirt and stayed there.

With a fierce smile on her face, his baby shot off her big guns. She took out at least three more people, and then she went empty.

Spike bent down and retrieved the soldier's machine gun. Precisely at that moment someone else sprayed the area with most unfriendly fire. The bullets narrowly missed the top of Spike's skull as he flattened himself behind the dead soldier, turning the corpse on its side to increase the surface area.

"Dru!" he shouted.

Then more bullets flew fast and furious, torrents of them like English rain. Spike covered his head with his hands, shouting, "Bloody hell!"

A bullet pierced the back of his left hand. It hurt. A lot.

He dodged right, then zigzagged wildly, glancing about for escape, then finally throwing himself through a dingy, dirty window.

He slammed into a deserted room. The floor was filthy. Rolling in muck, he stood and darted out of the window frame and pressed himself against the farthest wall.

His hand was bleeding, but him being a vampire and all, he could work around it.

Outside, across the alley, Dru screamed. Spike clenched his teeth and balled his right fist. In that moment, as waves of rage and helpless fury roared through him, he transformed. His face became sharp and angled, his teeth, fanged and razor-sharp. His eyes glowed.

She screamed again. He went into overdrive, casting about for weapons in the half-light of the darkened room. He was in some kind of storehouse. Against the opposite wall, there were several cans of what might be petrol. On the floor, mixed in with pieces of wood and rotten bits of newspapers, the occasional rag.

Directly beside him was a portable cooking stove. But more important, a pack of matches. Ironically, they were from the café they'd just fled.

All he needed was a bottle.

Which was summarily thrown the broken window.

"Thanks, mate," he murmured.

He dropped to his stomach and crawled over to the bottle, ignoring the cuts in his hands as the shards of glass bit into his flesh. He grabbed the bottle, rolling over to avoid the fresh scattershot of bullets.

For the first time a stroke of luck: There was kerosene in the cans.

As quickly as he could, Spike sloshed the bottle full. He grabbed one of the rags and stuffed it inside, trailing a decent length out the top.

Some thoughtful soul had left a pack of matches

beside the stove. Spike lit the dry end of the rag, then hurled it back out the window.

A chorus of shouts rose up, followed by a fairly decent explosion. While that was going on, Spike snuck a peek out the window.

What he saw horrified him. They had strung Dru up by a lamppost, and they were trying to set her lovely dress on fire. She was clutching at the rope around her neck and kicking furiously. His firebomb had burst perilously close to the dainty bare toes of the left foot of his beloved.

"Dru," he whispered hoarsely.

Her eyes were bulging; she was clutching at the rope.

It was then that he saw that they were dousing her with water from small bottles—probably holy water, then—and rubbing her feet and legs with something. The stench came at him: garlic.

They were attempting to poison her on top of everything else.

He threw back his head and growled savagely. The sound was lost in the shouts and jeers of the mob as they tortured his poodle.

He ran back to the cans of kerosene. He began unscrewing their lids and throwing them out the window. Most of the crowd had forgotten about him; he avoided the few potshots aimed at him and kept at his business.

Halfway through dumping the kerosene, he found one more empty glass bottle.

"Yes, yes!" he exulted, kissing the bottle.

Suddenly someone shouted. Someone else answered. He looked up.

They were pointing to his puddle of kerosene and looking not so very delighted.

Some of the buggers began shooting at him. Others hurled bricks and stones. Plus a half-eaten piece of bread, which he strangely found rather insulting.

He filled the glass bottle with fuel, stuffed in a rag, and made a kamikaze leap out the window. Like someone in Manchester United, he hook-kicked the bomb. It went up, up, and the barbarians, realizing what it was, began to scatter.

The ones who didn't, Spike plowed into. He slammed his fingers under the breastbone of one short, pudgy man, ripping it free as the man contracted into a ball of pain. Another, he slammed in the Adam's apple. He thrust his elbow into the gut of another, then pushed him as hard as he could; the toppling fellow knocked over two or three others, who went sprawling.

The bomb had by then landed, and the pools of flammable liquid were going up like Roman fountains. Spike clawed and bit and fought his way to Dru as the fires raged. Her poor little feet were raw and bloody; her skin where the holy water had touched it were burnt black.

She stared down at him, her lips moving, no sound coming out.

"Hold on, baby!" he shouted.

He grabbed a gun from someone, shot that person with it, and then aimed it at the rope hanging above her head. He missed it by a mile. Tried again. Another mile.

He grabbed a Russian soldier and gestured. "Shootsky," he ordered the man, his fangs at the man's neck in case the bloke got the bright idea of shooting Dru.

The soldier was smart. He understood exactly what Spike wanted, and on the first attempt he shot her down. Spike's pet landed in a fragile heap like a wispy, broken moth. Spike ran to her, but not before he tore out the throat of the Russian soldier and threw him to the ground. As soon as he made sure Dru was all right, he was going to commit a bit of a massacre.

No sense leaving any of them alive.

No sense whatsoever.

One thing was for certain: It was time to leave off searching for Angelus. Now, if he could just convince Dru of that, they both might actually live to see a few more sunsets.

He figured that would be a more difficult task

than killing all these bleedin' goulash-eaters. But if any man was up to the task, it was Spike.

So: No more Angelus. As far as Spike was concerned, the bastard was dead.

He would never tell Dru, but the fact was, Spike realized he was just fine with that.

In fact, he bloody well hoped it was true.

Angelus was trouble.

ACT THREE

Chces li tajnou vec aneb pravdu vyzvédéti
Blazen, dité opily clovéc o tom umeji povodeti.

"Wouldst thou know a truth or mystery,
A drunkard, fool, or child may tell it thee."
—Romanian proverb

Angel reached Tina's apartment half on instinct and the other two-thirds on adrenaline. Which, theoretically, should not have been coursing through his body at the moment. But he was literally dizzy with worry for her.

He should have stopped her. Dodged the lamp more quickly; hell, tackled her if he'd had to. If anything had happened, if something . . .

He couldn't even go there.

So he ran down the hall.

Her door was ajar, and his hopes exploded.

He tried to tell himself that in her haste to leave, she'd left the door open.

But he knew.

He steeled himself as he went inside, but he knew.

There she was, on the floor, next to the sofa bed. Stone dead.

Her throat torn open, her blood drained.

Still, he raced to her and checked her pulse. There was none, and he had known there wouldn't be.

He had failed her.

He might as well have killed her himself.

A vampire did this, he thought. *Why be surprised?* There were practically as many vampires in Los Angeles as there had been in Sunnydale. But Tina . . . and all that evil and monstrousness . . .

He stopped and saw her blood on his hands.

He stared at it, riveted. Beyond tempted. It called to him, sang to him. Human blood. He remembered the taste, the wonder of it. Couldn't deny that he had yearned for it, just as Doyle had insisted.

Before he realized what he was doing, he thrust two blood-covered fingers into his mouth.

He reeled; his eyes clamped shut at the overwhelming sensation—far more than taste, or smell, or sustenance—it was what he was; the blood was the life—his life and soul; it was his being.

Oh, oh, more—

His eyes snapped open.

What had he done?

He was sickened. Lurching, he stumbled to the bathroom, sick, and turned the water on hot, hotter than he could stand. He thrust his hands under the nearly boiling gush and washed them, scrubbing over and over until they were nearly raw.

How could he have done that to her? The last act of betrayal of her sad life.

Committed by the one person whom she really could have trusted.

Or should have been able to trust.

He kept scrubbing, remembering how he had tried to decontaminate himself after his change back from Angel into Angelus. After Buffy's love had reactivated his curse.

Spike and Dru had laughed so at him. Looked at him askance now and then, utterly horrified at the notion that one of their own had gone renegade. Killed his own kind, siding with the humans. Since there was little honor among vampires, they accepted him back; Dru with arms wide open, Spike initially delighted, but never quite losing his suspicion that Angelus was not there to stay.

Spike had been too right.

Or had Angelus stayed after all? Did that demon

lurk inside, biding his time, waiting for just the right moment to make a rebid for ascendance?

Angel looked in the mirror, which offered no reflection. But he could see, behind him on the floor, Tina's body. She bore silent witness to his memories, and his regrets, and to his despair.

I must never assume I'm the good guy, he thought. *It could have been me, literally, under the right circumstances.* He was stunned that even now he stared at the wound on her throat with fascination. Even now.

He crossed to the phone, his gaze never leaving her face. Silently he dialed 911.

It must have been like this after I killed Jenny, Angel thought. *And Giles was there, watching every impersonal, uncaring moment of it.*

Tina's apartment bustled with activity. A coroner studied Tina's body while two detectives combed the place for clues. A forensics assistant was dusting for prints.

All this, Angel could see from his vantage point on a neighboring rooftop. He waited, still and silent, as her body was bagged and taken away.

Then he turned, grim, stepped up on the roof ledge, and leaped.

He landed on another rooftop far below and disappeared into the darkness.

He had so much to make up for.

He wasn't certain eternity would be long enough to do it in.

Russell Winters lived in an enormous, ostentatious fortress. Iron gates secured the stone wall that surrounded it; a guard was stationed in a kiosk next to the gates at all hours of the day and night.

When you were who—and what—Russell Winters was, you took precautions.

Which was fine.

Russell Winters could certainly afford them.

He sat back with satisfaction in his office and watched the video Margo had shot at the party of Tina. His place of business was large and spacious, and filled with the tools of his trade: computers, huge monitors, paintings, an empty desk, and thick drapes secured against the daylight. Enormous piles of material shielded him from that famous Southern California sunshine.

From this nest of vast luxury, he kept his finger on the pulse of the world economies. He had more information pouring into this room than some of the large Wall Street brokerage houses received from all their branch offices. He had more money than many small nations. With that money he had bought himself a wonderful existence here in Los Angeles. Beautiful artwork. Exquisite clothes and cars.

Beautiful people.

The intercom buzzed and William said, "Mr. Mc-Donald from Wolfram and Hart is here, sir."

Ah, another of my precautions.

"Show him in, William."

William, the butler, escorted Lindsey McDonald from the foyer of Russell Winters's mansion toward the study. It was a trip Lindsey had made many times, and yet it never failed to impress—and inspire—him. Uniformed maids polishing and cleaning; everything speaking of incredible wealth and power. Lindsey aspired to it.

He would do whatever he could to get it.

"Hello, Mr. Winters, sorry to disturb you at home," he said politely as William bowed out, leaving them alone.

Mr. Winters rewound the video. It was the girl. The young, beautiful, dead girl.

"A man is only disturbed to see someone from his law firm when he brings bad news," Mr. Winters said offhandedly, his eyes on the video. "Am I going to be disturbed, Lindsey?"

"No," Lindsey assured him, staying poised and professional, although he was very proud of all the good things he had done for Russell Winters in the last twenty-four hours. "The Eltron merger is a go. They caved on everything after you . . . negotiated with their C.F.O. We'll bring the final drafts to your office tomorrow."

Mr. Winters took that in. "Yet you're here today."

Lindsey nodded, glancing at the girl on the screen.

Mr. Winters said, "She had something, didn't she." He rewound the tape again. "It's a little sad when you kill them so young."

Lindsey stared at the girl, then impassively opened his briefcase and brought out a sheaf of documents. He showed them to Mr. Winters.

"Actually, you haven't seen her in several weeks," he informed his firm's client. "You were in conference yesterday with your contract lawyers when the unfortunate incident occurred. And we've located a witness who's telling the police he saw a dark-complected man with blood on his hands fleeing the scene."

Winters was impressed. "Am I paying you fellows at Wolfram and Hart enough?"

He shoots, he scores! "Yes," Lindsey said calmly. "See you tomorrow."

Concealing his sense of triumph, he returned his papers to his briefcase while Mr. Winters continued watching the video. New scenes from the same party splashed across the monitor.

"Who's this?" Mr. Winters asked, interest in his voice.

Lindsey looked at the monitor. He and Mr. Winters were looking at a vivacious young woman with a terrific figure and lustrous dark hair. Very lovely. Lovelier even than yesterday's. Stunning cheekbones. And what a smile.

Thoughtfully he closed his briefcase and asked, "Should I alert the firm that this young lady may constitute another . . . long-term investment?"

Mr. Winters studied the girl's image. "I don't think so. I just want something to eat. That reminds me. Short Brew Food Supplies four hundred thousand shares."

Lindsey made a mental note.

Around Mr. Winters, he always took notes.

Not that he ever let on.

The soul of professionalism, that was Lindsey. Face blank of ambition, devoid of greed. He was the perfect lawyer for a man—a thing—in Mr. Winters's position. Discreet, loyal, nonjudgmental. Whatever Mr. Winters needed the law to do, the law would do.

Lindsey McDonald would see to that.

The Los Angeles Underground had been a controversial mass transportation project from the get-go. At least two construction workers had died. It had gone so over budget that some sections of it cost five hundred million dollars a mile.

With the huge digging machines that were

brought in, the construction workers uncovered fossils that were eight and a half million years old. In North Hollywood a digging crew unearthed the original tile floor of the building where the treaty which ended the California phase of the Mexican-American war was signed. In the new tunnels beneath Union Station thousands of artifacts from Los Angeles' first Chinatown had been found.

Rumors were rife that many other things had been dug up; things people could not identify: strangely shaped bones; bizarre objects currently labeled as "Asian Miscellania."

It appeared more and more likely to Angel that Sunnydale had nothing on Los Angeles.

He sat alone in the darkness of one of the subterranean construction tunnels. The distant rumbling of the subway was like the warning growl of a massive animal.

Doyle approached slowly. Obviously, he knew about Tina's death.

Dully Angel said, "She wanted to go home."

Doyle was sympathetic. "Yeah."

"I'd like to compliment the Powers that Be on a terrific plan. I really saved the day."

"It didn't work out," Doyle agreed.

" 'It didn't work out?' " Angel felt a rush of anger. "Tina *died*. A vampire ripped her throat out. Was that the grand scheme?"

"No one controls the future. You're a soldier. You fight." He gestured. "Sometimes you lose."

That was true. He had lost before. Buffy had lost before.

Even the best weren't the best every time.

"I . . . I cared about her," he said, the words coming with difficulty. "And it wasn't enough. I was supposed to help her—"

Doyle cut him off. "I don't know. Maybe she was supposed to help *you*. Maybe she had something to give you."

"Like what?"

"Grief."

Angel looked at him, considering.

"There's a particularly nasty vampire out there. Rich, protected, can do any damn thing he wants. He's killed, and he'll keep on killing till someone's mad enough to take him down."

He got in Angel's face. "What you need, boy, is a bit o' therapy. You have great pain. It's time to share it."

Angel considered. How did you share pain like this? It was private. More important, it was necessary for his soul.

Wasn't it?

Rumania, 1898

In the winter of 1898 Angelus took a coach through the Carpathian Mountains, bound for a rendezvous with Spike and Drusilla. Eavesdropping on the ghost stories the prunish old chaperon was murmuring to her delectable charge, a delicate young heiress, he grinned and wondered what she would think if she knew what kind of monster sat reading a French novel across from her.

The second night on the journey the rear axle of the coach snapped. The coach veered precipitously close to the edge of a deep chasm. The women were like hens, shrieking and flying about inside the coach, and it was only by taking command of the situation that Angelus managed to escape unharmed. He told them to join him on the opposite side of the coach, their combined weight serving as a counterbalance. He climbed out first (naturally), urging the horses to move right, using their weight. He assisted the fainting ladies out and managed, with the horses, to drag the vehicle a bit away from the chasm.

The driver had been thrown off, his neck broken on impact. Though Angelus assured the ladies he could drive a coach, or preferably lead them out on horseback, the females returned to their blind panic. The women's shrieks and yowls were so intense that they eventually attracted a pack of wolves.

The creatures of the night surrounded the three travelers and stared with hungry, glowing eyes as the snow began to fall.

The horses reared and screamed, and the wolves gathered their muscles, preparing to spring. When Angelus stood between them and the horses, they backed down in submissive postures.

As for the two women, they clung to each other and began praying and making the sign of the cross, until Angelus could abide it no longer. He tore out the throat of the older woman, which caused the wolves to attack the horses. He was able to save two of them, but to his regret, the wolves took the opportunity to drag off the young heiress. Smears of her blood in the snow told him where they'd gone, but he figured there'd be nothing, if anything, left worth retrieving.

So he made a fire and sat beside it for a time. The snowstorm was worsening, and he wondered what he should do for shelter when the sun rose. He considered the carriage and decided that if nothing else, it would keep the sun off him. What a cramped, boring refuge that would be. Perhaps the heavy snowfall would be sufficient to keep the morning brightness at bay.

The fire crackled, and he sat drumming his fingers. Now and then a wolf would venture near, but sensing what he was, they all kept their distance.

An hour dragged by. Then the snow fell too heavily to see his pocket watch. He felt rather ridiculous. He wondered if Spike and Dru had already reached Budapest.

Then, in the swirls of white, a fair-headed woman approached. She was singing sweetly, and when he cocked his head and squinted through the storm at her, she said, "Hello, precious."

Darla. His wonderful Darla.

"Nice weather we're having, eh?" he quipped.

It was as if they had never parted. She came to him and kissed him, and they curled together in the snow, oblivious of the freezing weather. Her eyes were a crystalline blue, like the frozen Siretul River. Her lips, pink and lustrous. She was more beautiful than he had remembered.

"Where have you been, you naughty man?" she chided.

"On my way to Budapest," he informed her.

"Alone?" She touched his face. He transformed for her. And she for him.

"Not anymore."

They rolled in the snow and cavorted like the wolves that watched them.

The wolves that knew far better than to attack these splendid predators.

❖   ❖   ❖

The snow stopped falling midday the next day, and the sun came out. Angelus and Darla hid in the carriage, amusing themselves by catching up.

The horses survived the storm, and the two vampires mounted them, riding bareback.

They traveled on to Budapest. Spike and Dru met up with them. There was an earthquake, of all things, and in the delicious chaos amongst the human population, the four picked the fruit right off the vine. It was a vampire bacchanalia.

It was what being a vampire was all about.

After that, Dru spoke of Spain and wanting very much to go there. Darla refused to go; she had very bad memories of the Spanish Inquisition, not a happy time for creatures of the night. Despite the focus on the Inquisition's barbarity in dealing with human beings accused of witchcraft and heresy, truth was the monks and priests had significantly reduced the power of evil in the world.

Darla demanded to stay in the Balkans. Spike seized the moment and suggested he accompany Dru to Spain alone—accent on alone, thank you very much—while Angel "squired his sire."

So it was decided, with Drusilla acting a bit crestfallen. They would meet later in the year in Bucharest.

But, of course, they never did.

Darla and Angelus returned to the Romany

woods, ranging over the countryside like the wolves that sang to them at night.

It was in this time that she introduced him to the Master, an ancient vampire whose name in life had been Heinrich Joseph Nest. Angelus never saw him in other than his true face, and it was more demonic than his own, very pale, almost ratlike. Angelus envied him his looks.

Darla was clearly one of the Master's favorites, and he took an instant liking to her bloodchild, Angel. Eager to impress him with her judgment, she recounted many of Angelus's exploits to him. Soon Angelus was numbered among the Master's inner circle, and he was known to say Angelus was the most vicious creature he'd ever met. He promised Angelus that come the day when his plans for domination of the world came to fruition, Angelus would sit at his right hand.

In return, Angelus vowed loyalty and devotion to all the Master's causes. It was a promise not undertaken lightly, and one he fully intended to keep.

At the time.

The idyllic year passed, moving into summer. Angelus had agreed to meet Spike and Drusilla in September, and it was now August.

Perhaps Darla meant to keep him there, with her

and the Master and the court. He never had a chance to ask her.

One warm night they had laughed and loved together, wearing exotic silk kimonos one of the Master's children had brought home from a rampage through Japan. Her cold skin beneath the silk stirred him; her kisses inflamed him.

Then she led him through the woods for a midnight hunt. Some Romanies had arrived in the daytime and chosen to park their wagons on the vampires' hunting ground.

"What sport," Angelus said quietly.

"Look there, precious."

Darla pointed at the most beautiful human woman Angelus had ever laid eyes on. She wore a full, striped skirt and a billowing white blouse, her splendid shape silhouetted by a tight waistcoat laced beneath her bosom. She was barefoot, and on each ankle, chains of gold coins jingled. Her black hair was loose and free, and her face . . . ah, the moon herself.

"For you," Darla said generously. "Knowing as I do that you appreciate the finer things in life."

They smiled at each other.

Then they parted, to dally with their prey. Darla would find a handsome young man, of that Angelus was certain. Meantime . . .

"Hello," he said softly, coming upon the exquisite Gypsy as she strolled alone by the river.

She started. The frightened look on her face did not diminish as he stepped from the shadows. Her eyes darted left, right.

He gestured to his mouth. "I'm thirsty."

She blinked. *"Pai?"* she asked in a soft, pleasing voice.

"Pai," he agreed. He smiled kindly. He could hear her heart; it was thundering. She was mortally afraid.

"I'm staying with friends, and I wandered off," he said in English. "I've been walking through the forest for hours."

With that, she took off. Angelus watched her go, highly amused, terrifically enchanted. He decided then and there to woo her.

The look of horror and betrayal on her face when he took her life would make the kill all the sweeter.

And it did; it was the most wonderful kill of his life up until that point. She had come to him and said, in the halting English he had taught, "Angelus, I love you."

Then she had kissed him, quite sweetly. Contrary to common prejudice, Gypsy women, while passionate, were chaste until marriage.

Since such a marriage never could, and never would, take place, Angelus decided that this was the moment he would celebrate his triumph over her.

He was careful to allow her to see his transformation; more careful still to give her a head start before he threw her down and tore open her throat.

What Angelus had not realized was that he had been seen murdering the girl, whose name still eluded him.

He had a rival, a brash Gypsy who had adored her, but considered himself unworthy of her. She was the clan's favorite daughter, and he was only one of many cousins.

That didn't prevent him from loving her, and from wondering who it was who had claimed her heart.

Ashamed of himself, he had decided that very night to follow her.

And he had seen.

At the Gypsy camp the girl was lovingly laid out. Her burial gown was the best the clan possessed. The keening of grief was a delightful ode to Angelus's savagery. On the path back to the Master's underground lair, he stopped to listen. He had not expected them to find her so quickly. Now he was torn between pretending to be drawn to the camp by the sound, to see what was amiss, or returning to the Master's court to boast about his accomplishment.

*   *   *

"*Mulo*," the Gypsy woman murmured. It was Gypsy for a dead person associated with uncleanness. It meant vampire.

She wore a shawl and had painted the seal on her forehead. She waved her hand over the Orb of Thesulah and began the incantation:

Nici mort nici al fiintei,
Te invoc, spirit al trecerii
Reda trupului ce separa omul de animal
Cu ajurtorul acestui magic glod de cristal.

Not dead, nor not of the living.
Spirits of the interregnum, I call.
Restore to the corporal vessel that which separates
us from beast.
Use this orb as your guide.

In the forest a horrible pain ripped through Angelus. He stumbled, looking over his shoulder, trying to see what had attacked him. There was obviously nothing in front of him.

He fell to his knees, gasping.

Never had he felt such terrible agony. He was being ripped apart inside, by an unseen enemy. He ran through the woods, heedless of his direction.

He fell again, and this time he lost awareness for a brief moment.

As he got to his knees, groggy and bewildered, an old Gypsy approached and hovered over him.

"It hurts, yes?" he said in English. "Good. It will hurt more."

Angelus was dazed. "Where am I?"

The man was contemptuous, bitter, filled with rage. "You don't remember. Everything you've done, for a hundred years, in a moment, you will. The face of everyone you killed—our daughter's face—they will haunt you and you will know what true suffering is."

"Killed?" Angelus repeated, confused. He thought to himself, *Where's Sandy Burns? Where's that charming woman I followed into the alley—*

"I don't—"

In a flash the memories rushed over him—Darla; his change, his rampages, the tortures he had inflicted on his victims. Drusilla. Servants, ladies, men, children, babies.

The Gypsy girl, so sweet and trusting—

He had done it all.

"Oh, no, no." His guilt was unbearable *"No!"*

As the Gypsy man looked on with satisfaction, Angelus began to scream.

BUFFY

"She was my first love. I'm not saying it was an easy relationship. But it was real. I guess I knew it couldn't last. You see, Gypsies, they pulled a funny on me. If I ever experience a moment of true happiness, if my soul is ever at peace, I'll lose it, become a monster again. So I had to leave. I wanted to shut the world out. No more love, no more pain, no more demons."

And that was what it all boiled down to: the grief had a name. Buffy.

Darla had tempted him. Drusilla, he had corrupted. Faith, he had failed.

Tina was dead. Tina, whose trust was shattered too many times. Who ran from the one person she should have been able to run to.

But Buffy . . .

Every thought he'd had, every memory he had relived since returning to Los Angeles, related to his love for the Slayer.

He had fallen in love with Buffy that very first time he had seen her. He remembered telling her that once; something about how she held out her heart, and him wanting to hold it against his chest. It had actually been very gross, and they'd chuckled over it.

Thinking of it now, he smiled wistfully. He wondered about her constantly. Tried to imagine what she was doing.

The pain washed over him in waves.

Buffy . . .

He remembered their night, their only night; and as he did so, he realized he was finally saying goodbye. The memories would start to fade.

That hurt worst of all.

The memories would fade.

Sunnydale, 1998

The blue demon called the Judge had tried to burn them, kill them for their humanity to charge up his evil-force batteries. Together, in the strange almost-telepathy they shared, Buffy and Angel had created a diversion—dropping a pile of TV sets on the floor—which had also, luckily, broken through the floor.

Voilà, instant escape route.

To neither's joy, they landed in the sewer. Silently, no need for talk, they slogged through the muck until they found an opened utility door. With an economy of motion a Green Beret would envy, they darted inside and shut the door behind them.

Spike and Dru's followers landed soon after. The two were hot on their trail, but they couldn't see the nearly invisible seams of the closed door, and moved on.

After waiting a few more minutes than they thought were necessary, Buffy and Angel reemerged into the tunnel. As good city planning would have it, there was a ladder nearby, which led to the street overhead.

The rain was coming down in sheets, washing the street to a slick, black shine as Buffy pushed the manhole cover out of the way. She was shivering almost uncontrollably by the time Angel got out and took a quick mental survey of their surroundings.

"Come on," he bellowed over the thunder. "We need to get inside."

They slogged through the weather to his apartment. Ever chivalrous—might have had something to do with when he was born—he unlocked the door and let her enter first.

The dim light made Buffy look colder as she stood

in the center of the room. Across the wall, just above his bed, the reflection of the rain down the window made a strange kinetic sculpture.

Angel pulled off his duster and turned to her, stroking her shoulders. "You're shaking like a leaf," he said.

She nodded, shuddering violently. "C-cold."

"Let me get you something." He went to his dresser and got out a bulky white sweater and a pair of sweats. They smelled as if they'd just come out of a warm dryer.

Handing them to her, he suggested, "Put these on and get under the covers. Just to warm up."

A little hesitantly, maybe feeling shy and self-conscious, Buffy walked over to his neatly made bed. She stood in front of it for just a second before she sat down on the mattress, the bundle of fresh clothes in her arms. The coverlet and pillow cases were scarlet.

The rain continued its drizzling pattern on the wall. Distant thunder rumbled.

Lightning crashed.

Angel came to her and faced her. When she looked up at him, he realized he was staring at her. He said, "Sorry," and turned around.

Still, she was very near. He could almost smell her, the wetness of her hair, the tantalizing freshness of her skin. Buffy always smelled good, though she herself would beg to differ.

She was awkward as she unbuttoned the drenched cardigan of her twin set. As she drew out her left arm, she grunted. There was something wrong with her shoulder.

"What?"

"Oh, um. I—I just have a cut or something," she murmured as she finished taking off her sweater. He knew she knew he wanted to look at her, and she was behaving with touching shyness.

"Can I . . . Let me see." His voice was gentle but firm. He would brook no refusal; if Buffy was injured, he wanted to know.

"Okay." Modestly she arranged the sweater across her front so that she was covered. He was moved by her innocence. This was a Buffy he had glimpsed on several occasions, but to see her here, in his room, on his bed . . . it gave him an overwhelming sense of protectiveness toward her.

He sat behind her on the bed as she turned to show him the wound on her back.

His fingers touched her shoulder as he pulled the spaghetti strap of her camisole down. His touch was infinitely gentle and tender. Both of his hands moved over her upper back, "It's already closed," he said hoarsely. "You're fine."

Neither moved. Buffy was trembling harder. Angel swallowed hard. He was certain he could hear her heartbeat, or was that his own pulse magically restored, racing as his arms cradled her?

She turned, leaned into him. Breathed him in. Tears welled. He was overcome by her nearness, by the fact that he had almost lost her. That tonight he had thought he might never see her again.

Echoing his thoughts, she said, "You almost went away today."

His fingertips stroked her arm as he held her, tension in his body. He was being careful of her; he was struggling against what was taking them both over: the fear, and the need. He reminded himself constantly of how young she was, how innocent in these matters. How could she be otherwise? She spent most of her waking hours fighting monsters, not kissing boys.

He said, "We both did."

She started to cry. "Angel, I feel like . . . if I lost you . . ." She caught her breath. "You're right, though. We can't be sure of anything." She moved her lips to the side of his face and wept.

"Sssh. I . . ."

She opened her eyes, waited. Looked at him. "You what?"

"I love you."

And when he said it, her eyes brightened in wonder, though the tears were still there. He loved Buffy. He knew it was what she had longed to hear, for such a very long time; and yet, there was tremendous sorrow in his words, and in knowing what he had barely dared to dream. Angel loved her, and now, knowing that, he had so much more to lose.

"I try not to, but I can't stop," he said brokenly.

"Me, too." Her voice cracked as she was overcome with emotion. "I can't, either." She pressed her nose against his.

They kissed. The kiss grew. They were crossing a bridge; they were going somewhere together they had never been before. Buffy's heart pounded, as if with the knowledge that this kiss was the beginning of something much bigger; this was a seal, and a promise, and a first step.

Their passion grew. Angel was starving for the taste of her; he shook with the need of her.

Panting, he pulled away. "Buffy, maybe we shouldn't. . . ."

"Don't. " She touched his face, held it. "Just kiss me."

Their lips met again, and again.

Angel drew Buffy down into his bed. *She's so beautiful*, he thought. *She feels so amazing. Her skin, her hair* . . . He breathed her in. The scent of her, the satiny softness of her neck, her shoulders. Her hands, caressing him.

Oh, Buffy, Buffy, let me lose myself in you.
Love me.

As they melted into each other, Angel soared with joy. For the first time in two hundred and forty-two years, he had hope of heaven.

The thunder rumbled and crashed.

Angel bolted awake, unbelievable pain ripping through him. White-hot agony seared him, body and soul.

He panted, fighting it. It was an ancient pain, and he knew what it meant. He knew what was coming, and he was desperate to stop it. He clutched the sheets, heaving, as Buffy slumbered beside him.

No, no, not now . . . it can't be. . . . Buffy . . .

Everything was shattering. As he convulsed, he clung to one thought: He had to put as much distance between her and himself as possible.

Protect her . . . oh, my darling, oh, Buffy . . .

Protect her from me . . .

Angel dressed and stumbled out into the storm, into the wildness of the night. He clung to the hope that it would stop, that it would not happen. But as he fell to his knees, he knew: His soul was being torn from him once more.

"Buffy!" he shouted.

She was the last thought of the man who loved her.

And then the pain was silenced.

But it still grew.

Sunnydale, 1998

Buffy knew he was trying to end the world. She knew how. He didn't care if she knew why.

All he knew was that he had to kill her as quickly as possible, or everything would be lost.

She had come for him armed with a powerful sword given to her by Kendra, the Slayer Drusilla had recently killed. As they battled—unknown to him—Willow was invoking the Spell of Restoration of Souls on his behalf.

But he didn't know that; and he wouldn't have wanted it, in his state. All he wanted was to kill Buffy so she couldn't interfere with his plans to send every single living human being straight to Hell.

He fought her with all his strength, and at one point he thought it was over. So he had taken the time to toy with her—always Angelus's weakness when dealing with his enemies; the temptation to add a little soupçon of cruelty was too sweet to pass up.

In the garden of the mansion he shared with Spike and Dru, who had come to roost in Sunnydale, the Slayer was sprawled on the flagstones. She was boxed in; every move she tried, he mirrored, and he played the sword near her face, loving every moment of her torment.

"That's everything, huh?" he'd asked with mock

concern. "No weapons, no friends. No hope. Take all that away and what's left?"

His words hit home. She looked exhausted, and terribly sad. She shut her eyes.

He lunged, shooting his arm out, the sword straight at her face.

Without opening her eyes, she slammed her palms together over the blade, stopping it an inch from her face.

"Me," she said.

She jerked the sword back, knocking the hilt into his face, and kicked him hard in the chest.

He fled into the mansion, landed hard on the floor. He got back up and she charged him, sword in hand, pounding at him as he fought back with his own sword; driving him back.

She knocked his sword out of his hand, cutting him in the process.

He stood before her, spent and beaten.

At that moment, in the hospital, Willow finished the ritual to restore his soul to him.

In incredible pain again, Angel fell to his knees.

Buffy was about to behead him when he looked up at her.

She must have seen the glow of his soul, but even

after he called softly, "Buffy?" she took a step back, supremely cautious.

"Buffy, what's going on?" he asked, looking around. "I don't remember. Where are we?" For he had moved Dru and Spike into the mansion after he had lost his soul.

Buffy's voice cracked as she said, "Angel?"

He saw her wounds, said, "You're hurt."

He went to her and took her arm. He folded her into his arms..

"God, I feel like I haven't seen you in months. Buffy, everything's so muddled."

Later, he would know that she could see the vortex that would pull the world into Hell growing in the mouth of the stone demon behind him. But at that moment he had no idea what was going on.

He only knew that she was very troubled, and that she was holding on to him as though she could never, ever let him go.

"What's happening, Buffy?" he murmured.

"Sssh," she said. "It doesn't matter."

She kissed him passionately and said, "I love you."

"I love you . . ." His voice was filled with wonder: Were they to be together after all, then? Was it a dream, or could it really be true?

Then she had said softly, "Close your eyes."

He had obeyed, trusting and happy.

And she had thrust the sword through his chest, pinning him to the stone demon.

The vortex emanating from its mouth pulled him straight into Hell.

He was tortured and tormented for the earthly equivalent of five hundred years.

And then, for some reason, he was brought back.

Back to this world, yes, but not to Buffy's arms.

Never to Buffy's arms again.

And so, after a few failed attempts to build a simpler relationship with her—a friendship, even a hatred, even nothing—it became clear that Hell had followed him back.

Now he belonged to Los Angeles. Where, according to Doyle, his job was not only to protect, but to minister to. To care for. To understand.

He sighed heavily.

It wasn't Hell, but close to it.

Purgatory, then.

And if there was redemption to be found there, then someday . . .

He closed his eyes . . .

Someday there *would* be a heaven.

ACT THREE,
CONTINUED

The sign by the plate-glass window said STACEY'S
GYM SUPPLIES.

It was still there after the thug came crashing
through the window.

Angel had Tina's abductor—whose name, he supposed, was Stacey—by the throat, pressed up
against a wall. He had to keep reminding himself
that he couldn't kill this guy. He had information
Angel needed to get the monster who'd taken Tina's
life.

"Where does he live? How much security does he
have?"

Despite his predicament, Stacey was contemptuous.

"Listen, hotshot," he told Angel. "Whatever she
was to you, you better forget it. You have no idea
who you're dealing with here."

Angel tightened his grip around Stacey's throat.

"Russell? Lemme guess: Not big on the daylight or the mirrors, drinks a lot of V-8?"

It was obvious that Stacey was surprised Angel knew his boss was a vampire. Still, he grunted, "You get in his way, he'll kill you, he'll kill everyone you care about."

Angel's grip grew tighter. And tighter. Stacey nearly fainted.

Angel said, "There's nobody left I care about."

After Angel left, he found himself thinking about someone who had made the same claim. She had believed she had no one, and that knowledge had hardened her, ruined her.

Her name was Faith, and she had seen some pretty awful things in her life, even before she became a Slayer. Witnessing the death of her own Watcher had marked her soul.

She had fled to Sunnydale in search of Buffy, and the two had teamed up to kick vampire butt.

But from the start Faith had been channeling a darker side of slaying—enjoying the power and the perks, acknowledging no authority. It all caught up with her one night in a dark alley when she accidentally killed a human. A line was crossed. And that awful knowledge drove Faith straight into a doomed alliance with Sunnydale's mayor.

Angel, who couldn't save himself without Buffy's help, tried to repay the favor by saving Faith.

Angel's Mansion, Sunnydale, 1999

Angel captured Faith and handcuffed her to the wall. She was a powerful Slayer; he had seen her in action, and he knew he had to be cautious around her.

He said to her now, "I know what's going on with you."

"Join the club," she said sullenly. "Everybody seems to have a theory."

"But I know. What it's like to take a life. To feel a future, a world of possibility, snuffed out by your own hand. I know the power in it." He looked at her closely. "The exhilaration. It was like a drug for me."

She sneered at him and yanked on her chains. "Yeah? Sounds like you need some help. A professional, maybe."

He shook his head. "A professional couldn't have helped me. It stopped when I got my soul back. My human heart."

"Goody for you." She huffed at him. "If we're going to party, let's get on with it. Otherwise, could you let me out of these things?"

Angel was not going to be distracted. Or deterred. "Faith, you have a choice. You've tasted something few ever do. To kill without remorse is to feel like a god—"

She obviously didn't want to hear it. She started to struggle. "Right now all I feel is a cramp in my wrist. Let me go!"

"But you're not a god," he persisted. "You're not much more than a child. And this path will ruin you. You can't imagine the price for true evil."

There was a flicker in her eyes. Something he had said hit the mark. But still, she would not yield.

"Yeah? I hope evil takes Mastercard."

"You and me, Faith, we're a lot alike."

She snorted. "Well, you're kind of dead. . . ."

"Like I said. A lot alike."

"Sorry, buddy. I'm alive and kicking. In fact, I've got a bodily function that needs attending to pretty quick here."

Angel was insistent. He knew he was reaching her. He knew she was almost hearing him.

"You're not alive," he said. "You're just running. Afraid to feel. Afraid to be touched."

Part of her reacted to his words. But she averted her gaze and muttered, "Save it for Hallmark. I have to pee."

"Time was," he continued, "I thought humans existed just to hurt each other."

Faith looked back to him now. She was silent.

Finally, he thought gratefully. *I've struck a chord.*

"But then I came here," he pushed. "And I found out that there were other kinds of people. People who genuinely wanted to do right. They still make mistakes. They fall down. But they keep trying. Keep caring."

There was a long beat. She was taking it in, clearly wanting to believe. Angel saw it. He moved to her, speaking to her from the heart.

"If you can trust us, Faith, it can all change. You don't have to disappear into the darkness."

But she had. Poor Faith, she had.

So who do I think I am, he wondered, *that I think I can help anyone at all?*

And then he thought: *It doesn't matter what I think. Just like Buffy. She didn't think she would be a good Slayer. But she's the best.*

Ironically, Buffy had been exiled from Los Angeles to Sunnydale. He had been forced to leave Sunnydale for L.A. They had traded places, in effect.

Something clicked in him.

I really am supposed to be here, he thought.

With a pang he finally left Sunnydale behind. The memories would begin to fade. He knew that now. He would miss them.

But he was home.

❖   ❖   ❖

Cordelia, in sweat pants and a T, kept her lotus position as she took deep breaths of cleansing energy. *In, green. Out, red.*

A new self-help book, *Meditation for a Bountiful Life,* sat beside her. She just knew that aligning her chakras with the vibrational resonance of the book's positive message was going to pay off.

"I am somebody." She took a deep breath.

"I matter." Another.

"People will be attracted to my positive energy and help me achieve my goals."

She glanced at her phone machine. The message counter registered a big zero. The last call she'd received was that awful one from Joe. She hadn't even had a date in over two weeks.

Wouldn't they just laugh their heads off back in Sunnydale if they could see me now?

She remembered how snotty she'd been to Buffy about Angel. Always trying to snag him, very insulted when he proved unsnaggable. And then, of course, there was finding out he was a vampire:

Sunnydale High, 1997

Buffy and Willow were sitting in the girls' bathroom at school, yakking or cutting class or whatever losers did. Cordelia came in to wash her hands and check her makeup, and she noticed the lack of conversation that occurred as soon as she showed. So she decided to give Buffy something new to talk about.

"So, Buffy," she began, in a sweetly accusing voice, "you ran off last night and left poor Angel by his lonesome. I did everything I could to comfort him."

"I bet," Buffy replied.

Hah. Score one for Queen C.

"What's his story, anyway? I mean, I never see him around."

"Not during the *day*, anyway," Willow chimed in, like that was some big deal or something.

"Oh, please don't tell me he still lives at home," Cordelia groaned, suddenly wondering if a honey like him could really be such a dork. "Like he has to wait for his dad to get back before he can take the car?"

Buffy said helpfully, "I think his parents have been dead for, um, a couple hundred years."

Cordelia wasn't exactly paying attention. "Oh, good." So it took her a moment to process Buffy's little ha-ha joke. "I mean—*What?*"

"Angel's a vampire." Buffy seemed to take such delight in so informing her. "I thought you knew."

For a moment, Buffy had her. Then Cordelia said, in a sarcastic tone, "Oh. He's a *vampire*. Of course. But the cuddly kind. Like a Care Bear with fangs."

Willow piped up. "It's true." The narc's narc, that was Willow Rosenberg.

Cordelia gave Buffy a knowing look. "You know what I think? I just think you're trying to scare me off because you're afraid of the competition. Look, Buffy, you may be hot stuff when it comes to demonology or whatever, but when it comes to dating, *I'm* the Slayer."

Yeah, right. Here I am, slaying away. Knockin' 'em dead. So busy I don't even have time to sit alone in my crummy apartment and even miss Xander, for heaven's sake.

She looked back down at her book, reminding herself that positive was magnetic, and negative was repellent.

"I am right where I'm supposed to be and not *dying for something to eat!*"

She hurled the book across the room, sitting there on the verge of tears. She was starving. She was frightened. She wanted to be rich again. She hated all this struggling.

The phone rang.

Cordelia jumped, startled, and picked it up. She said, using her new positive tone of voice, "Hello. This is Cordelia Chase."

"Cor, it's Margo," said the voice on the other line. Cordelia thrilled. "You were such a hit at my party."

Yes, yes, yes. "Thanks. I had a great time. I want to have you over to my place"— she winced—"as soon as I'm done redecorating."

"Well, guess who saw my videotape of the party, and guess who wants to meet you?" Margo asked in a leading way, which meant it had to be someone important. Someone who could help her.

"A director?" she asked excitedly. "A manager? An assistant to an assistant who's ready to spring for lunch?"

"Russell Winters."

Cordelia could scarcely believe her ears. "The investment guy?"

"Oh, Cordelia, he's a lot more than that," Margo said, clearly amused. "He helps people get started in their careers. He knows everyone and . . . he wants to meet you tonight."

Cordelia's eyes widened. "Tonight? Well, let me check my calendar." She was so excited she thought she might pass out. Still, she made herself wait a beat, as if she actually had to consider the entire matter, before she answered.

"I'll have to cancel a couple of things, but I'm sure I can—Wait." She took a little breath. "I don't have to have sex with him, do I? 'Cause I couldn't . . . I'm nearly positive that I couldn't—"

"No, no," Margo assured her on the other end.

"He just likes to help people. I don't think he enjoys sex at all."

Cordelia said happily, "Oh, good!"

"He'll send a limo for you at eight."

And it wasn't a joke. The limo actually came. A long, sleek, black shark like the ones that traveled the highways starting around the northern end of Orange County. The closer you zeroed in on Los Angeles, either coming south or north, the more limos you started seeing. And now she was in one, and it wasn't last year's prom or anything. It was real life.

She rode in the very back, in plush comfort. Queen C triumphant. She drank mineral water and munched some nuts. Delicious, protein-filled, energy-laden nuts. She couldn't help but hum a happy, tuneless melody to herself. Now, *this* was the way it was supposed to be.

The limo glided toward the sprawling mansion. The enormous building was like a castle, one of those places where people live in a room for years and no one realizes they're there. It was beautiful, perfect, oozing wealth and wonderful networking possibilities. Talk about being connected. She could scarcely believe her good fortune. But she had to believe. Absolutely believe.

The limo approached a huge iron gate. There was

a guard in a little building who hit a button. The gates swung open.

As the car glided through, Cordelia intoned, " 'People will be attracted to my positive energy and help me achieve my goals.' *Oh, yeah.*"

Happily she popped a nut into her mouth.

Behind the limo, the large gates swung shut with a clang.

ACT FOUR

In Angel's apartment Doyle looked on, obviously impressed, as Angel wrapped up an array of gear: timer, detonators, plastique explosive, a small set of tools, rope, and a few odds and ends.

"Wow. You're really going to war here." Doyle looked thoughtful. "Guess you've seen a few in your time."

Angel surveyed his materiel. "Fourteen. Not counting Vietnam. They never declared it."

Doyle nodded. "Well, this is good. You're taking charge and fighting back." He looked curiously down at Angel's collection of stuff. "Do you really need all this?"

Angel did a quick mental run-through. Yes, he needed it all. If he could have carried anything else—a grenade launcher, if it would have helped—he would. Whatever it took, this was Russell Winters's last night on earth.

He felt another pang as he thought of Tina and said simply, "A Girl Scout told me: Be prepared."

"Well, best of luck." Doyle looked very concerned and extremely sincere. "I got some fairly large coin riding on the Vikings tonight, but I'll be with you in spirit."

Angel stopped him. "You're driving."

Doyle registered a wee bit o' shock. "What? But . . . no. No, no. I'm not combat-ready," he insisted. "I'm just the messenger."

"And I'm the message," Angel retorted.

In Russell Winters's mansion Cordelia told herself giddily that she should have brought a canteen and a compass. It was that big. That fabulous. That gorgeous.

Wow.

He has a house as big as a football field.

Wow.

He has a butler.

He wants to meet me.

Wow.

She wanted to pinch herself, but she didn't want to leave a mark. Not that he would care. Okay, he might care. But he wouldn't care because he expected her to do anything with her arms. And he wouldn't want to look at her arms. He didn't care about anything about her, right? Except whatever it was that had attracted him to her. Her laugh? Her smile?

She hadn't even realized Margo knew him or would send him the tape of the party, and she didn't know what he looked like, anyway. To be honest, when the butler had answered the door, she'd almost chimed in with "Hi, Mr. Winters."

The butler moved along silently, and Cordelia was sure he could hear her heart pounding. Finally, finally, things were going to start being positive. Life was good. The future was good. Because she mattered.

Eventually she was ushered into what had to be Russell Winters's home office. Spacious, elegant, and reeking of lots of money on interior design, it was bigger than her entire apartment. She had a brief moment where she imagined herself giving her thirty-day notice on her rat trap, and then there he was, rising to greet her.

"Hi. I'm Russell," he said in a friendly voice. "Thank you so much for coming."

He waved the butler away. The man silently left.

Cordelia thought, *Show time*. She figured she should still try to impress him. You never really knew when you had clinched the sale.

Not that she was selling anything. No way. Except her image. And her positive energies.

"So," she began, smiling brightly. "Nice place."

She gestured. "I love the curtains." *Wow, there are tons of them.* "Not afraid to emphasize the curtains."

He shrugged somewhat modestly. "I have old-fashioned tastes."

"I grew up in a nice home," Cordelia assured him. "It wasn't like *this*, but we did have a room or two we didn't even know what they were for."

He smiled.

"Then the IRS got all huffy about my folks forgetting to pay taxes for, well, ever. They took it all."

"And Margo says you're an actress," he said. "That's going well?"

"Oh, yeah, it's great." *Sound positive. Radiating positive energy is not lying.* "I've had a lot of opportunities. The hands in the Liqui-Gel commercial were almost mine by like one or two girls, and, well . . . it's not everything I . . ."

She trailed off, her facade crumbling. She looked at him and felt forlorn, wondering what he would require of her.

Wondering if she would have the courage not to do it, especially if it was something really icky.

Some vampires live in basements, and some live in aeries, Angel thought as Doyle rolled the convertible to a stop beside the guardhouse in front of the Winters mansion. It reminded Angel of the stately country homes of long-ago Galway and the surrounding countryside. Most of them were museums now, or part of the Public Trusts scheme.

Angel climbed out and approached the guard. The guy sat before more monitors than a Las Vegas casino security department. They showed the property from several angles—entrance, rear, east and west sides. Bushes, trees. Lots of trees. And ghosts.

No, make that marble statues.

"Hi. I think we're lost," Angel said to the unsmiling guard. "I'm looking for Cliff Drive—hey, what ya' watching? Is that the Vikings?"

Angel leaned over and looked at the monitor that showed his car and the front of the house. He reached out, grabbed the transmitting wire from the video camera on the gate, and ripped it out. The monitor went snowy.

"Hey," the guard said angrily. "What are you—"

He was fishing for his gun as Angel knocked him out.

Angel said to Doyle, "Tie him up. I'm out in ten minutes or I'm not coming out."

"Ten minutes," Doyle repeated.

Angel grabbed his gear and bolted.

At the wall Angel leaped, grabbed the edge, and pulled himself upright. He ran along it into the night.

Finally he reached the section closer to the house. He stopped and crouched low as an armed guard walked the property. The man didn't appear to know anything unusual was going on. He was just making his rounds.

He turned a corner, and Angel ran on along the wall. Then he leaped, landing on the roof of the mansion. He scrabbled over the roof and jumped again.

He landed in the side yard. After checking for guards, he attached plastique and the detonator to an auxiliary generator. *That'll make a nice explosion.*

He headed along the corner of the house to the fuse box and started working on it next.

He's so understanding, Cordelia thought hopefully. *Such a great listener.*

She sat with Russell Winters in his study, and he was all ears as she opened up to him far more than she had intended.

"I've tried really hard, you know? Usually when I try at something I succeed right away. I just thought this would be . . . but I don't have anybody. I don't even have any friends out here."

"Now you know me," he reminded her. "And you don't have to worry anymore."

She looked down. *He can't just be nice,* she told herself. *Otherwise, this would be just like living in a movie, and I have left all that kind of stuff behind me right where in belongs, in Sunnydale.*

"What do you want me to do?" she asked.

"Just tell me what you want."

She tried to collect herself, knew she was trying to stall the conversation. Everything she wanted, he could give her. A career . . . but she had talent, she knew she did. She needed help getting started. Just a tiny break.

A break wouldn't cost too much, would it?

She crumbled a little. "Oh, God. I'm sorry." She wiped her eyes. "Here I am getting all weepy in front of you—" She looked around for a mirror. One mirror. One single mirror.

"I probably look really scary. I finally get invited to a nice place with no mirrors and lots of curtains and hey, you're a vampire." She looked at him.

He was caught off guard. "What? No, I'm not."

She raised her chin. "Are, too."

He moved away from her. "I don't know what you're talking about."

"I'm from Sunnydale," she announced proudly. "We had our own hellmouth. I know a vampire when I . . ."

Oh, my God, what am I doing?

". . . am alone with one in his fortress-like home and you know I'm just so light-headed from hunger I'm wacky and kidding!" She laughed. "Hah hah . . ."

Off his look, she added weakly, "Hah."

Uh-oh.

❖　　❖　　❖

163

Angel finished rigging the third auxiliary generator he'd attached to the wall.

Good, he thought. *This puppy will blow right on cue.*

Then he heard footsteps. It was another guard, walking around the corner.

It was only with split-second timing that Angel was able to pull himself up out of the line of sight of the guard. As soon as the guard passed the generator and disappeared from view, Angel dropped quietly to the ground once more.

He set the timer he had attached to the generator for ten seconds.

Why give Winters a chance to get out safely? Better to send him to hell asap.

Stay calm, Cordelia ordered herself. It was her new mantra. If she could have breathed, she would have done anything to create some more positive vibrational resonances. She needed all the help she could get.

"You know one of my very dearest friends is a vam—do you prefer 'night person'?"

Russell said pleasantly, "Truth is, I'm happy you know. Means we can skip the formalities."

All hope of calmness fled. In the vacuum, pure terror rushed in.

"Please," Cordelia begged.

He growled and morphed. She registered shock as she realized he was far more hideous-looking than any other vampire she'd ever seen, before she screamed and fled the study.

She got to the main foyer, then ran up the stairs. Panting, she flew as fast as she could, but he was right behind her. Easily he grabbed her, and Cordelia just about lost it.

Then there was the unmistakable sound of something exploding three times—or maybe three things exploding once each—BLAM, BLAM, BLAM!

And all the lights went out.

The room was dark, save for shafts of moonlight. The grotesque vampire looked around in bewilderment; Angel could see the arrogance, the creature's assumption that he was invisible and would always be spared from the consequences of his actions.

"Russell Winters."

Angel stepped out of the shadows.

"Angel?" Cordelia cried hopefully.

"What do you want?" The vampire sounded alarmed, if angry.

Angel could barely restrain himself from attacking. *I didn't realize Cordelia would be here,* he thought. *But it makes sense. She was at the same party with Tina and me. Cor must have known her.*

He said, "I have a message from Tina."

The vampire blanched slightly at the name. So Angel had it figured right: This monster had been the one. It preyed on young girls, feeding their hopes, feeding its need for sadistic pleasure, then . . . simply feeding.

He thought of Tina's blood in his mouth. The thing that pretended to be Winters had drained it all away. But they had both fed off her. Under their masks, they were basically the same.

The realization sickened Angel to his core.

Winters recovered and said, "You've made a very big mistake, coming here."

"You don't know who he is, do you?" Cordelia taunted Winters. "Oh, boy, are you about to get your ass kicked!" She was gleeful, if still frightened. Angel hoped he wouldn't let her down.

The two vampires charged each other, trading a couple of quick, vicious punches. Russell knocked Angel hard enough for Angel's reflexes to go into action: His face changed, and he revealed himself to be, at the core, one of Winters's brethren.

"One of us?" Winters said, surprised. "Didn't you get the owner's manual? We don't help them. We eat them."

As Spike would say, "Our raison d'être."

From his ratchet device beneath his sleeves, Angel produced a stake and launched himself at

Winters. Winters held back, getting the better of Angel and holding back his stake.

The doors burst open and two guards ran in, guns drawn.

Winters shouted, "Kill her!"

The two men pointed their guns at Cordelia. Angel threw Winters out of his way and catapulted in front of her as the guards fired.

He took the bullets, registering for only the briefest of moments the pain as he tackled her and sent them both over the stairway railing. They hit the floor and bolted for the back door.

Sure, and that's a few bullets too many, Doyle thought to himself as he sat behind the wheel of Angel's car.

Yet there were more.

"That's it. I'm gone."

He threw the car into gear and burned rubber down the street. The smell of the tires exactly equaled the smell of his fear.

He was scared, and not proud of it. And Angel was back there, risking undead life and limb to stop the evil Doyle had, essentially, led him to. . . .

"Dammit."

He gave the wheel a sharp yank, catapulting the convertible into a big 180. The wheels squealed like pigs but everything held.

He barreled toward the huge metal grates. "Yaaahhhhhhhh!" he shouted, imagining himself as Mel Gibson in *Braveheart*. Only that boyo had been Scots, and everybody knew the best demons around were Irish—look at him and Angel.

No, don't look at all—

The car gained tremendous speed and rammed into the gates.

Which held just fine, thank you very much, unlike the front bumper and hood of the car, which crumpled like a cheap toy. Maybe even one made in America.

Doyle sat stunned for a moment. Then he said, "Good gate."

He backed the poor, smoking car off the gate. The dear creature was lurching but still running.

And then dropping down in the space Doyle had made were an extremely beautiful girl and Angel, who appeared to be very badly wounded.

They climbed into the car.

Of Angel's prized possession Doyle began to explain, "I had a little . . ."

More gunshots!

"We'll talk later," Doyle suggested.

He hit the gas, and they lurched away.

Angel's shirt was off. Cordelia had explained to Doyle how to use the forceps to extract the bullets, but Angel supposed Doyle had never had first aid—or anatomy—and it hurt maybe worse than getting shot in the first place.

Unfortunately, there were a lot of bullets. Ergo, a lot of pain.

Cordelia said anxiously, "We can't actually kill you unless we put a stake through your heart, right?"

Clenching his teeth, Angel gritted, "Maybe you should get one."

"Got it." Doyle dropped a bullet casing next to three others he had extracted.

Cordelia was vastly relieved. *"Finally.* I thought I was going to faint while barfing."

Angel smiled grimly as they bandaged his chest. That was the Cor Angel remembered from Sunnydale: always so worried about other people.

"So it's over, right?" Cordelia demanded. "We're both going to be okay. You put the fear of God in that Russell guy. He's not gonna come looking for me, right?"

Angel traded looks with Doyle. *Great minds think alike.*

Doyle looked just as worried as Angel was.

It was a tower of downtown power, and the fancy brushed-steel sign in front read RUSSELL WINTERS ENTERPRISES.

Inside, in the main conference room, Lindsey sat

at the foot of the table, closest to the door. Lawyers lined the sides of the long, polished table, stone-faced and professional, and Mr. Winters himself sat at the head, facing away from the bank of tinted glass windows.

Lindsey's briefcase, embossed with the *Wolfram & Hart* logo, sat opened beside him as he removed the first set of documents.

"The Eltron mutual trust binder is ready for your signature," he announced.

He handed the docs to a smart young woman lawyer on his right. They went down the row of lawyers to Mr. Winters.

"Also, we spoke to our office in Washington this morning," he continued, realizing with pride that all eyes were on him. It was a reaction he hid, however. "The new tax law we lobbied will knock three percent off gross taxes and kick up profits accordingly. We were pretty pleased with that down at the firm."

That's enough boasting, he cautioned himself. He passed down some more docs.

"As to the intruder who broke into your home last night, the local authorities have no information on him, but we have several top private investigators—"

The door crashed open and a tall, dark-haired man walked in.

"—looking into his whereabouts," Lindsey finished evenly.

Mr. Winters said, "I believe we've located him."

Lindsey moved to the man, who looked a little ragged.

He regarded the man—Angel, he believed his name was—and handed him his business card. "I'm with Wolfram and Hart," he told the vampire. "Mr. Winters has never been accused of and shall never be convicted of any crime. Ever. Should you continue to harass our client, we shall be forced to bring you into the light of day. A place, I'm told, that's not all that healthy for you."

Lindsey smiled.

Angel glanced down at the card, now in his own hand, and then at Mr. Winters.

Mr. Winters said, "This is the big city, Angel. It works in certain time-honored ways. You don't belong here. If I were you, I'd get out while I could. Tell Cordelia I'll see her real soon."

Mr. Winters smiled, holding Angel's gaze. The stranger looked around, clearly a little defeated by the realization that Mr. Winters had the stronger position—legally and in every other sense of the word.

Angel said, "I guess if you're rich and powerful enough, got the right law firm, you can do whatever you want."

Lindsey's client looked smug. "Pretty much."

"Can you fly?" Angel queried.

Mr. Winters's smile wavered. Then, before anyone could do anything to stop him, Angel lifted his foot, positioned it on the chair between Mr. Winters's legs, and pushed with all his might.

As Lindsey gaped in shock, Mr. Winters, in his chair, rocketed back fast, crashing into and through the wall of glass at his back.

He went flying out into the sunlight. As he fell, shrieking, he burst into flame and burned to vampire dust.

Angel, just out of the direct sunlight flooding in through the broken window, stood watching. Lindsey and the ranks of stone-faced lawyers were behind him.

Angel drawled, "Guess not."

Angel turned to leave, pausing to slip Lindsey's business card back into the lawyer's breast pocket as he exited.

Perfectly deadpan, Lindsey said, "Well."

Maintaining his composure, he snapped his briefcase shut. The others followed suit, calm and cool.

There would be other rich and powerful clients. The city was filled with vampires.

All kinds of them.

After all, this was Hollywood.

Russell Winters Enterprises: The chair cascaded, then smashed into the ground and bounced, a few dusty ashes sprinkling down in its wake.

◦　　◦　　◦

It was still day, but Angel wasn't sleepy. Exhausted, yes, but he knew this day he would not rest.

Angel sat by himself, by the phone. After a moment he thought, *Hell with it,* picked up, dialed, and waited.

Buffy's voice poured into his heart, "Hello? Hello?"

Angel hung up. He was certain of one thing: He had not been sent to Tina to learn the true meaning of grief after all.

Her name was still Buffy.

And the memories weren't going to fade any time soon.

Doyle walked into the room. "What happened with Russell?"

Angel replied, "He went into the light."

"Yet ya don't seem in a celebratin' mood." Doyle looked mildly intrigued.

Angel shrugged. "I killed a vampire. I didn't help anyone."

"You sure o' that?"

From overhead came the sound of a scream.

The two bolted upstairs.

And into Angel's office, to find the old desks and file cabinets dusted and moved into the inner and outer office spaces. Cordelia, wearing one of Angel's shirts, sleeves rolled up, had been dusting and shoving furniture around.

"Aaaaghhl! Cockroach!" she informed them wildly. "In the corner. I'd say a bantamweight."

Doyle went to check.

Cordelia turned to Angel.

"Okay," she said, "first thing, we have to call an exterminator. And a sign painter. We should have a name on the door."

"Okay. I'm confused," Angel drawled. "Again."

Cordelia smiled. "Oh, Doyle told me about your little mission and all and I was saying, if we're gonna help people out, maybe a small charge, a fee, you know, something to help pay the rent, and my salary. . . ."

He stared at her, speechless.

She went on, "You need someone to organize things, and you're not exactly rolling in it, Mr. I-was-alive-for-two-hundred-years-and-never-developed-an-investment-portfolio."

His mind was parsing her quick sentences. More important, his heart was warmed by what she was offering.

Still, he asked, "You want to charge people?"

"Not everybody," she assured him. "But sooner or later you'll have to help some rich people, right?" She looked to Doyle. "Right?"

Doyle said, "Possibly."

"Hand me that box," she ordered Angel. "So I figure we'll charge based on a case by case analysis, but with me working for a flat fee."

Angel regarded her for a moment, still taking everything in. For a moment her bravado slipped, and she looked at him meekly.

"I mean, that is, if you think you could use me. . . ."

There was a beat. Then Angel handed her the box, smiling gently at her. She took it happily and left for the outer office, calling over her shoulder, "Of course, this is just temporary, till my inevitable stardom takes effect."

Good old Cor.

The closest thing I have to my old life.

Doyle said, "You made a good choice. She'll provide a connection to the world. She has a very humanizing influence."

Angel wasn't fooled for a moment. "You think she's a hottie."

Doyle was embarrassed about being seen through. "Oh, she's a stiffener, can't lie about that. But she could use a hand."

Angel said, "True."

"There's a lot of people in this city need helpin'," Doyle added, as if seizing the moment.

Angel let him have that moment. "So I noticed."

Doyle was pleased. "You game?"

Angel could feel the small smile creep onto his own face.

❖   ❖   ❖

In the dark night, standing like a sentinel, Angel looked down on the city. The whole of Los Angeles was laid out before him. His to guard. His to protect.

There was much he didn't understand. Much to figure out.

Much to feel.

Way too much to feel.

Los Angeles was the city of dreams. And heartbeats. And tears.

As he looked up at the sky, he wondered if Buffy was doing the same. If those were thoughts she had.

If he would ever see her again.

If it would ever stop hurting.

But for now he would serve his penance. He would find redemption, not by grace, but by good deeds.

The traffic washed down the highways. The glass buildings shimmered.

The moon was full and warm and golden; hanging low in the sky like a nightlight in the room of a little child.

Angel was alone; he had really always been alone. Anything to the contrary was just a wish on a falling star.

Or was it?

Doyle watched, as he often did.

"There's a lot of people in this city need helpin'," he had told Angel. "You game?"

Are you in, Angelus, the One with the Angelic Face, or are you out?

Angel stood in the breeze, his coat flapping like wings.

Then he turned and looked directly at Doyle. He'd known the demon had been there all along.

He said to Doyle, "I'm game."

About the Author

USA Today bestselling author Nancy Holder is the author of 42 novels, including 13 projects for *Buffy the Vampire Slayer* and *Angel*. A four-time winner of the Bram Stoker Award, she has also written 200 short stories, essays, and articles. She lives in San Diego with her daughter, Belle.

Bullying.
Threats.
Bullets.

Locker searches? Metal detectors?

Fight back without fists.

MTV's Fight For Your Rights: Take A
Stand Against Violence can give you
the power to find your own solutions
to youth violence. Find out how you
can take a stand in your community
at FightForYourRights.MTV.com.

fight for your rights:
take a stand against violence

BUFFY

THE VAMPIRE
SLAYER™

IMMORTAL

She cannot die.
Strike her down, but like the night she will always
come again.
And she will bring forth the end of Man....

Has Buffy met her match in an
immortal vampire?

The first Buffy hardcover
by Christopher Golden and Nancy Holder

Available from Pocket Books

... A GIRL BORN
WITHOUT THE FEAR GENE

FEARLESS™

A NEW SERIES BY
FRANCINE PASCAL

A TITLE AVAILABLE EVERY MONTH

From Pocket Pulse
Published by Pocket Books